I0533896

The First Interceptor

- An Intercepting Fate Prequel -

Cameron Stewart Miller

Chapter 1:
Ain't That A Conk In The Head

There was nothing quite like the incredible sight of Sellea City. From the top of a jagged skyscraper, Chase watched the hectic flow of traffic both on the ground and in the sky.

Pollution slipped from the cars on the streets below into the air above, giving the traffic in the sky an ominous appearance.

"I hate this song," Chase said as he brought a finger to his temple.

There was a small chime, and the visor attached to his head projected a dull orange interface.

As he took another sip of his horrid mina-gunk smoothie, Chase scrolled through the music his visor had on offer. He chuckled at the sheer volume of tracks available on such a small piece of tech.

"Ain't tech the coolest—" he scrolled to the rock hip-hop fusion section and picked an old favourite, before swiping the interface away.

The difference between the two types of traffic that stretched across the city disappointed Chase. The cars on the ground stretched on for what seemed like forever, while the traffic in the sky was at least manageable.

He hoped a time would come when the city would stop being divided. Creating class divisions between the rich, middle class, poor, and ultra-poor only fostered hatred throughout the city.

A hatred that Chase could hear as the drivers below honked and shouted at one another.

BOOM!

An explosion deep into the heart of the richest section of the city caught Chase's eye. In truth, it had to have caught most people's eyes with how high the blast had travelled. If there was any traffic in the air near the explosion, there was bound to be quite a bit of destruction.

Chase's visor started to ring.

She must have seen the explosion.

He gave his visor a tap. "Go for Chase."

"Tell me—you saw that." Marin said through laboured breaths.

"Sounds like *you* did," Chase chuckled. "I'm on my way."

"Could you just—not do anything stupid this time?"

"Hmm," Chase finished the last of his smoothie and tossed it aside. "Define stupid."

Chase stretched as he looked toward the cloud of dust that had risen in the distance. It could have been some kind of accident or tech malfunction, but he knew it was almost certainly something else.

Those violent creations.

"Need I remind you about the last time we ran into a bunch of bots? Where you—"

"Yeah, yeah, yeah," Chase looked down at his hand. "Don't punch the big hunk of metal. I figured it out the hard way, I don't need more reminding." He cupped his hands over his eyes to block the sun. "How far are you?"

"Five minutes—max."

"Tell you what—" Chase pulled a square disk from his jacket pocket. "Last one there—buys dinner."

"You're on. I'm always up for a free meal." Marin said before the call disconnected.

Chase closed his eyes and took a deep breath.

"Best part of my day."

He hadn't had much to look forward to since he finished up at the academy, but potential action against some bots was something he could always get excited about.

He took one last look toward where the explosion had occurred before he hopped off the roof of the skyscraper.

"WOO-HOO-HOO-HOOOO!"

The feeling of the rushing wind on his face was exhilarating. He imagined all the people looking out the windows of the building he'd jumped off. He might be traumatizing a few people, but it was the fastest way he had to get to the explosion.

His eyes fell on the sky traffic.

He needed to make sure he timed things perfectly or he'd be about as solid as that smoothie he had just finished.

As he crossed the line of the traffic, he tossed the square disk out in front of him. It morphed until it became Chase's baby—a sleek tech-cycle.

The grips of the handles were already warm as he pulled himself onto the bike. He'd put far more credits into his ride than he'd like to admit, but it was worth it. He had one of the nicest tech-cycles in the city, even without having all that much money to his name.

The traffic on the ground was getting a little too close for Chase's liking.

He flicked the starter and revved the engine to get it ready to go. Just before he smacked into the ground, Chase pulled up and hit the gas. The back tire of his ride smacked into the roof of a car as the tech-cycle swooped into the air.

"Sorry about that!" Chase yelled in response to the angry driver.

He maneuvered around and settled into the sky just above the line of traffic. It wasn't exactly—legal to ride around where he was in the sky, but it was an emergency situation.

As he sped across an intersection, Chase sighed.

If he managed to spot them—they'd certainly have managed to spot him.

Police sirens flicked on and a car sped behind him.

"You guys sure are nowhere to be found until it's the absolute worst time," Chase said as he sped up.

There was no way he was going to pull over.

He was far too busy.

A good ole fashion high-speed pursuit would be fun, and some backup on the scene would probably be helpful. With how big that explosion had been, there was bound to be a small army of bots attacking someone or something.

He weaved his way in and out of the sky traffic, switching between riding above and below. As he rose above the traffic, Chase spotted the source of the explosion.

There was a huge crater in the middle of a popular shopping section. The kind of place all the snooty people gathered to brag about the five-thousand credit shirt they just bought.

Three cheers for branding, right?

The cops were having a hell of a time staying on his trail, but to their credit, they managed to arrive at the scene of the explosion right behind Chase.

There was a brave bot separated from a larger group of bots.

The perfect target.

Chase put each of his feet onto the seat of the bike as he sped toward it. He eye-balled the range and flicked one of the tech-cycle's switches. It crumpled back into a disk as Chase shot forward, legs first, into the bot.

He nailed it with the flying dropkick and it went shooting backward into the group of larger bots, sending them all to the ground.

Chase hit the ground with a groan, "That's probably one of those stupid things Marin was talking about."

He was surprised he hadn't managed to hurt himself more. The only real pain he was in came from the sudden jolt to the ground, which drove all the air from his chest.

A hand thrust into his view. "That's exactly the kind of stupid thing I was talking about."

"How many did I get?" Chase took the hand and got to his feet. "Musta been at least ten."

Marin looked like she had just gotten her hair done. She had talked about getting her long black hair cut to a more manageable length—whatever that was supposed to mean in girl.

Apparently, that meant getting it cut to the point where there were only a few inches remaining on top. He wasn't the biggest fan of shorter styles like that, but it worked on her.

"It doesn't matter how many you got if you take yourself out of the fight right away," Marin rolled her eyes. "You got twelve of them."

He pumped his fist. "I'm standing aren't I?" He could feel a slight tinge of pain in his knees and ankles, but he wasn't going to admit that to her.

She scoffed, "Barely."

Chase took a look back at the police that had followed him as they piled out of their squad car. Rather than arrest him, they readied themselves for a conflict with the bots.

He gave Marin a cheesy grin. "You owe me dinner by the way."

"You only beat me by like—two seconds."

"A deal's a deal. I'm feeling something fancy. You can show off that—interesting—new cut to the world."

A bot rushed toward the pair, but they were ready for action. Chase pulled a knife from his belt and with the push of a button a thin orange blade shot out of its hilt.

Marin pulled a brand new crossbow from her back and aimed it at the bot.

Chase rolled away from the bot's incoming blade. "Where'd you get that?"

"I—" Marin baited a swing from the bot. She rolled under the strike and launched an arrow into its leg. "I picked it up this morning. You like?"

Chase kicked the bot's leg in from behind and as it fell to a knee, he drove his knife into its head. The hilt of the knife banged against the bot's sparking head with a deep CONK.

He pulled his knife back. "God, I love that sound—CONK!"

The bot fell to the floor motionless.

Zeal really needed to improve his designs.

Chased twirled the knife in his hands as he walked back to Marin. "I do like it. Where's mine?"

"You think I'm made of money?" Marin looked up at one of the many shining news drones that had flown in. "Something tells me I won't need a night out to show off my new cut."

The duo looked up at a nearby billboard displaying feed footage of the two of them standing around. It was annoying to be put on display for the world every time the Vanguard arrived to help, but at least the public could see that they really were trying to make a difference for the people of Sellea City.

"So that's a no to Shift?"

"You said dinner, not drinks and dancing."

"They do food too. I hear it's *almost* bearable."

Shots rang out and the duo turned to see a huge bot hop down from the roof of a building.

Chase chuckled at the half-hearted attempt from the cops. Bullets didn't do anything to regular bots, so why they'd think one that was nearly five times in size would be any different was anyone's guess. At least they were actually trying to help out.

That was better than most cops.

"You—uh—you know what the purpose of the attack is?" Chase asked as he stared at the huge bot.

Most people would have been terrified to be facing a massive robot, but it excited Chase. Rather than seeking a life filled with bland work, he was always willing to take his chances against stupid robots. Sure, it was way more dangerous, but at least it was more fun than an office job.

"Seem's like general chaos. It's probably some kind of diversion so Zeal can snag something nice and shiny from somewhere else."

"We gettin' any backup?"

A new arrow materialized on her crossbow. "The rest of the Vanguard is on the way."

"Sweet. Let's get to work." Chase rushed toward the big bot with Marin on his heels.

It launched a huge fist that they managed to dodge, but concrete debris flew into the air. There weren't any chunks big enough to do major damage, but even the small rocks stung as they smacked into Chase's body.

He jumped onto the bot's arm and drove his knife into it to keep a hold on it.

Marin launched an arrow at the bot's head. "This is more of you doing stupid things."

The bot waved an arm to shake Chase off.

"You know—you always—say I'm—stupid but—we always—seem to—win." Chase said as he inched his way up the bot's arm.

The bot lashed out with its other arm, sending a nearby car flying toward Marin. Chase watched her slide under it as it flipped toward her.

A situation like that probably would have scared the crap out of most people.

Not Marin.

That loveable psycho.

Chase made it up to the bot's shoulder as another arrow struck its head. "Can you watch it down there?" He asked as he stared at his close call.

"Where else am I supposed to target?"

"Gimme a sec!" Chase used the arrow to get to his feet.

He stood atop the bot's shoulder, praying that the cops wouldn't let some stray bullets fly his way. The officers were yelling, but he was too focused to take in anything they were saying.

In one swift movement, Chase raised his knife and slammed it down onto the bot's head with an even deeper CONK.

The bot's head sparked, but it wasn't going down.

"Stupid small knife," he said under his breath.

Chase pulled the arrow out of the side of the bot's head and drove it down into the top of its head. The bot started to spark as it finally dropped to the ground.

He pulled his knife and tried for the most graceful landing possible. Instead, he dropped hard to the concrete while leading with his face.

Grace was never Chase's thing.

Marin helped him to his feet again. "Don't even think about gloating right now."

"Why not? That was pretty—" He looked around at the wall of bots that surrounded them. "Oh. Makes sense."

The police couldn't risk firing at the bots for fear of

8

hitting either Chase or Marin. The last thing the police needed was the world to see them shoot two vigilantes trying to protect the public.

The familiar sound of tech-cycles revving down the street put a smile on Chase's face. "Get down!"

He pulled Marin to the ground as the scene got loud.

The bots started dropping one by one as a small wave of the Vanguard rushed in to even the odds. Bullets, arrows, and cyberweapons were flying in every direction.

Once all the chaos halted, they got back to their feet and looked around at all the fallen bots.

Marin brought a finger to her visor. "Nice work there, Tempo Squad."

Chase didn't hear the response, but knowing the members that made up Tempo Squad, it was probably something pompous and insufferable.

"Understood." Marin set her crossbow across her back. "We may want to get out of here before the cops get overly ornery—as usual."

"We can bask in our awesomeness for a sec." He dismissed her comment with the wave of his hand. "Looks like my stupid ideas work pretty well, huh?"

"Unless it involves you punching a metal bot," Marin said with a laugh.

"I'm never gonna live that one down, huh?" Chase set his knife back in his belt. "So get this, I thought up a name for these hunks of scrap metal." Marin raised an eyebrow. "Conks."

"Conks?" she asked. "What kind of a name is that?"

"Easiest way to bust 'em up?" He kicked what was left of the large bot's head and another CONK rang out. "Big conk on the head—Conks."

"Hmm." Marin didn't look enthused by the name.

"It'll grow on you. We can at least use it until we come up with a better name."

"Fine," Marin shrugged. "Conk it is."

A forceful push sent Chase to the ground. As soon as a knee met his back, he knew what was happening. "MARIN, GO!"

Chapter 2:
The Girl In The Disk

Marin faltered for a moment. Chase knew that she wanted to dive on top of the cop, but they both knew that would only result in both of them behind bars. She sprinted toward one of the few remaining Vanguard members and hopped onto his bike.

The rest of the squad rode away from the scene as the cops wrapped a pair of cuffs on Chase's wrists.

"You guys after an autograph?" Chase chuckled as they hoisted him to his feet.

"Speeding, riding in a no-fly zone, recklessly—" the cops began.

"Awesomely," Chase corrected.

"*Recklessly* engaging with a group of bots, *and* you're a high-ranking member of the Vanguard—you're going away for a long time, pal."

"Love it when you guys call me *pal*." Chase smirked at the cop. "You really think the Vanguard won't come for me?" The cop gave him a shove, but he kept teasing, "You know they've broken less important people out before."

Even though Chase was doing his best to exude confident energy, he was terrified. A guy like him couldn't just assault a pair of cops and try to get away. He'd end up behind bars even longer than he already was going to

"Shut it." The cop threw Chase against the side of his squad car. "We'll just have to make sure we take extra precautions with you then, won't we?"

"That's enough," A voice came from behind the officer. "Unhand him, now."

Chase cranked his neck around to see a young man with snow-white hair. He adjusted his bright purple suit jacket as he stared at the officer. It was clear that he was a resident of the high-end district of Sellea City. Bright clothes were a stamp that marked someone as rich.

"Griffin, sir—What are you—"

"Stop asking questions, and start listening to me," Griffin said.

The officer let go of Chase and unlocked his cuffs.

Griffin had to be pretty powerful.

There weren't many people in the city that could tell police officers what to do, and the cop seemed really nervous.

"Thank you. You may leave us now." Griffin's eyes fell on Chase. "I'd like to speak to Mr. Dyer alone."

The cop saluted. "Yes, sir."

The cops scrambled back into their squad car, and the rest of the officers on the scene did the same.

Chase was alone with a strange man in a bright purple suit. If he didn't know any better, he would have assumed he had just been saved by a pimp.

"Thanks—I think." Chase rubbed his wrists. "So, what can I do for you? Are *you* after an autograph? Looking to join the Vanguard?"

"Something like that. I've got some work for you actually."

Chase waved a hand. "Not interested." He gestured to the battered Conks. "I manage to keep myself pretty busy if you couldn't tell."

"Oh, I could tell," Griffin smiled. "I'd like to expand

your work."

The way Griffin carried himself made Chase uneasy. There was something about him that gave off a bad energy. Most people in the richer districts tended to give off a kind of arrogant energy, but his was nothing like that.

Griffin was just—weird.

"So—what? You want to make a donation to the Vanguard or something?"

"No. You see, my people have had their eyes on you for some time now."

Chase wasn't exactly under-the-radar around Sellea City, but people didn't tend to stalk him. At least, as far as he knew that was the case.

"Not gonna lie, that's pretty creepy," Chase said.

Griffin glared at him. "We've been watching your— heroics."

"What?" Chase pointed a thumb at the huge Conk he destroyed. "You mean me taking out the Conks?"

"That's an—amusing name you've given them," Griffin stifled a laugh. "That is exactly what I mean. Are you aware of what you've done for this city?"

"It doesn't really matter to me." Chase spotted his tech-cycle disk on the ground and pocketed it. "So long as I'm keeping people who can't defend themselves safe. That's all that matters to me."

"But that's *exactly* why you are of interest, Chase. You've destroyed more of these—Conks, you called them?" Chase gave a proud nod. "You've destroyed more of them than any other person in this city, and you haven't received a single reward."

"If my goal was a reward, I suck at my job," Chase shrugged. "I'm doing it because the cops are having a hell of a time trying to protect ordinary people from those things."

"Yet another reason why we're interested in you."

13

Griffin picked up an electronic component from one of the bots. "We believe we can expand your capabilities to the point that you could put a stop to all the destruction caused by the Conks once and for all."

Griffin sounded like he was full of crap. If the city couldn't even supply the cops with gear that could handle the Conks, why would they bother supplying random civilians?

"Like one of those superheroes from those old holos?" Chase asked.

"Exactly like that. The only thing we ask is that you leave the Vanguard." A sleek black limo flew in and landed behind Griffin. "If you'd be so kind as to step into my vehicle, I'd love to discuss this more."

"Yeah, no offence," Chase said as he stared at the limo. "I don't get into strange cars with even stranger people. I'm a fan of not getting molested. Also, why the hell would I ditch the Vanguard? You know what—I've got a date to—"

"Enough of this!" Griffin snapped. "You are one of four candidates needed for a specific project." Griffin took a breath to calm himself. "I can only get clearance to activate the project if you're *all* on board. Please, Chase. I need you to hear me out. That's all I'm asking."

The bad feeling hadn't left Chase. In fact, it was firmly situated in the bottom of his gut. It felt like Griffin was the grim reaper leading him toward his death, but Chase couldn't detect any kind of lie from him. He seemed so passionate and his pleas seemed so genuine.

There couldn't be any harm in at least hearing him out.

"Alright, Captain Exposition—you want to make me into some kind of hero—you got any proof of that?"

"Actually, yes." He pulled out a small square disk of his own, and held it in the palm of his hand.

"Is anything going to—"

14

The top of it lit up and a woman popped out of it.

"You must be Chase!" She spun around much like an overexcited child would. "I'm so excited to meet you!"

Chase stared at her. "You just—you just jumped out of a disk. How'd you—" He reached a finger out to poke her, but his finger phased through her. "What—?"

"Chase," Griffin stepped beside the woman. "I want you to meet Ayla."

She looked real. As real as Marin. She had jumped out of a tech disk, so there was no way she could be real, but there she was grinning away.

Chase waved. "Hi, Ayla." Ayla waved back and he turned to Griffin. "Uh—still wondering how she popped out of a disk. Answers please."

Ayla set her hands on her hips. "I'm an AI. More specifically, I've been designed to be *your* AI."

"My AI?" He raised an eyebrow. "What does that mean?"

Griffin held a hand up to Ayla. "If you come hear me out, we'll answer all of your questions—and more."

"Plus we can become life-long buddies!" Ayla added with an over-exaggerated swing of her arm.

The tech in Sellea City was pretty advanced, but nothing like Ayla. Chase had never seen a full-on person created and projected without the help of about a hundred different machines or a special room. Whoever Griffin was, he had some powerful people behind him.

"Hmm." Chase looked from Griffin to Ayla. "Ayla, what do you think? Is Griffin a trustworthy guy?"

"Well," Ayla looked at Griffin. "His taste in suits doesn't exactly make him look that way, huh? He just wants to take you to a government building to talk. I don't know why he's trying to be all cool and cryptic."

"So, you're with the government," Chase said.

"Ayla!" Griffin's eyes looked like they were ready to jump out of his head. "I told you we're not to tell anyone

15

why we're here."

"Yeah, but he'd find out eventually. Wouldn't giving him more information make him trust you more?" she asked.

Griffin brought a hand to his face. "Do the words *secret—project* mean anything to you?"

While Griffin was a weird guy, a person like Chase was always going to be enticed by any kind of secret project. If he'd just lead with that, the conversation might have gotten a lot farther a lot faster.

Ayla held up hand a to block him from her view. "I am so not appreciating the sass right now."

Chase just stared as the two bickered.

Most AI functioned in an incredibly basic capacity.

People couldn't even have a conversation with their visors. Even if Griffin was just some weirdo, finding out where tech like Ayla came from could be useful for the Vanguard.

Chase looked toward the limo. "I'll hear you out, but I'm going to share my location with someone just so you guys aren't tempted to kidnap me or something." He opened his visor and paired it to Marin's. "Oh, and no drinks, and no food." As he walked toward the limo, Chase took the hilt of his knife into his hand. "I'm not getting drugged by some weirdo in a purple suit."

Griffin pushed a button on the disk and Ayla shot back into it. "Excellent, I'm glad to—"

"No," Chase said. "I want to hear from Ayla as well."

Griffin followed with a smile as Ayla popped back out. "Of course."

"See?" Ayla skipped toward the limo. "He loves me already."

Chase settled into the ornate limo. It was weird that anyone ever needed a vehicle as big as a limousine. It could have housed a family or two from the slums without any problem.

Ayla flew over and sat next to Chase. "I'm so excited to actually get to talk to you. The people at the facility showed me all the incredible things you've done. What do you wanna know first?"

Chase could smell perfume radiating off of Ayla and he wondered just how advanced of an AI she was. "Well, for starters, one of you could tell me exactly what it is you want."

Griffin shut the door to the limo. "Ayla, would you like to tell him, or shall I?"

Ayla's clothes morphed until she was covered in a sleek high-tech suit. "We're going to make you into the world's first Interceptor."

Chase's face scrunched up as the limo took off into the city. "An Inter-what?"

Chapter 3:
The Facility In The Sky

Most of the dreary government buildings in Sellea City were in the section the Conks had attacked, but they were headed away from there. Wherever Griffin's office was, it had to be hidden somewhere.

He was pretty tight-lipped for most of the ride— until the limo took off into the sky.

"Not to poop on your party or anything, but I'm pretty sure we're in illegal airspace again," Chase said as he peered out the window. "Already had one close call with the cops today. I dunno if I'm interested in another."

Chase had a lot of questions that, much to his annoyance, both Griffin and Ayla wanted to wait to answer.

"Don't worry about it," Griffin said with a smirk. "The rules apply a little differently to a person like me."

Chase was the highest up he had ever been, and looking down on Sellea City from high above even the building he'd been perched on earlier was a sight to behold. It was the kind of sight he wished he could have experienced with someone like Marin for the first time, but an eccentric man with white hair and his hyper-advanced AI would have to do.

"You can put your knife away, too," Griffin

continued. "You aren't in any danger."

Chase looked at the hilt of his knife. "I'm just supposed to believe you?"

Griffin gestured to Ayla. "She's been created to be your partner, ask her if you're in any danger."

Chase sighed, "Ayla—am I, uh—am I in any danger?"

A pulse of energy flew out of Ayla and enveloped the entire limo. The hilt of his knife glowed bright green. Aside from the knife, not a single thing was highlighted. Every second, the tech that went into creating whatever Ayla was became more impressive.

"The only weapon on board is yours," she said.

"Okay," Chase put the knife back into his belt. "So the next obvious thing to mention—we're going into a bunch of clouds. Where is this facility supposed to be?"

Chase got a little fright when he noticed Ayla had sidled up beside him without making a noise. "What do you mean? It's right there." She pointed a finger to a cluster of clouds.

Chase raised an eyebrow. "Those—are in fact—just some clouds."

"Ayla, how about you uncloak the facility—" Griffin tapped his fingers on a window. "Just through the tech in the windows. The public doesn't need to know everything just yet."

Ayla nodded, "Sure thing, Griff." She held a hand up to the window in front of Chase and in place of the clouds, a huge floating facility appeared.

It wasn't attached to anything at all.

Somehow an entire series of buildings were on some kind of floating platform.

Chase moved around the limo, looking out different windows to see if it was some kind of trick, but it was visible through every window at every angle.

There it was.

A floating facility.

"That's not possible." Chase looked from Ayla to Griffin. "How long has that been there?"

"Hmm." He brought a hand to his chin. "I believe about five years? Is that right Ayla?"

"Five years next month," Ayla said.

Chase knew that there was no way they were telling the truth. In five years, Chase never spotted a single vehicle coming or going that high up in the sky. Although, the random decision to limit airspace for hover vehicles suddenly did make a lot more sense.

"Who knows about it?" Chase asked.

"Only those who need to know."

Chase glared at Griffin. "I'm getting tired of this cryptic shtick."

Ayla joined in with a glare of her own. "Me too. There's just over a hundred people that know about the facility—mostly scientists and armed forces."

"Thanks, Ayla."

"Anytime, my soon-to-be partner." Ayla held a hand up for a high-five, which confused Chase.

There's no way she could actually interact with the world around her, right? It really wasn't out of the realm of possibility. Ayla seemed so advance that maybe she had some kind of feedback built into her design so basic sensation of touch was possible.

Chase went for the high-five, but his hand passed right through. "Shoulda known."

"Gotcha!" Ayla laughed. "How advanced do you think I am?"

"I don't know," Chase sighed. "You guys aren't doing a good job of answering my questions."

"Hey," Ayla gave him a tender smile. "I promise everything's going to make sense once we get there, okay?"

"Okay."

"Trust me?"

It was strange having a computer program ask him if he trusted it. She was so advanced it was easy to forget that she wasn't really a person. She was right there in the limo sitting right next to him like any normal person could have been. An even weirder thought was how attractive she was.

"I trust you."

"Good, because we're here."

The limo pulled to a stop and Griffin opened the door, a rush of wind pushing its way through the vehicle.

Griffin stepped out with Ayla in tow. Chase started to follow but stopped when he spotted the slight gap between the limo and the facility. A controlled leap off a skyscraper seemed like nothing compared to the drop to the city below.

"Mind the gap," Griffin said as he continued toward a set of doors.

"No kidding," Chase said as he stepped onto the floating facility.

Ayla walked beside him. "I'm a big fan."

"Of me?" Chase narrowed his eyes and Ayla nodded. "Can a program be a fan of anything? Wouldn't you just be programmed to be a fan of me?"

"I take offence to that, Mr." Ayla stuck her nose in the air. "I'll have you know that I was designed for you, not designed to fawn all over you."

Chase couldn't believe he just offended a program.

"Oh. I—uh—I'm sorry. I didn't mean—"

"It's okay," Ayla laughed. "I know it can be kind of hard to wrap your head around things. Everything will make more sense once we get inside."

"You keep saying that—"

Ayla held a hand out and the ground underneath them started shifting them toward the door even faster.

Chase stared at her. "Here's a really good question,

what can't you do?"

"That is a good question! Hmm." Ayla brought a finger to her cheek. "Well, I have full control of this facility and I can interface with just about any tech, so I guess I just can't touch things—and I can't control people."

"Oh good," Chase said as they reached the door. "So basically omnipotence, minus tangibility."

"Well you know what they say, AI-liness is next to godliness."

Chase blinked at her.

Every attempt at AI he'd ever seen had the blandest personalities around. It was obvious that they were creations, but that couldn't be farther from the truth with Ayla. If she'd walked down the street past Chase, he wouldn't have stopped for a second—except maybe to check her out.

Griffin cleared his throat, "Chase, welcome to the facility. Soon it'll be home to you and your team, The Interceptors." Griffin pushed the doors open and the trio stepped inside.

The facility was gorgeous.

It was lined with huge windows that let in tons of natural light, but even with the beaming sun, the room felt cool. There were huge pillars that had lines of green data flowing through them and up into the ceiling. A beautiful gold fountain in the centre of the room tied it all together, but it felt like something was missing.

Chase cocked his head. "You guys know what's missing from this room?" Griffin raised an eyebrow. "A badass statue right in the middle of that fountain."

Ayla whirled around in front of Chase. "Maybe one day there'll be a statue of you there."

"I hate to get you down, Ayla, but I haven't agreed to anything yet. You know—since you guys *still* haven't told me anything."

Griffin rolled his eyes. "No one said you were this impatient." He led them into a smaller room with a couple of chairs and some holo-tapes on a table. "Wait here with Ayla. I'm going to go ahead and make sure everything is set up for the demonstrations. We'll be able to show you exactly what you're in for in one quick tour." Griffin tossed the disk Ayla had come out of to Chase. "That's for you to keep safe from now on."

Before Chase could ask any more of his millions of questions, Griffin had disappeared deeper into the mysterious facility.

"So what exactly is this?" Chase wiggled the disk. "Is this like your home—or your storage unit?"

Ayla looked around. "This is my home." She glared at the disk. "That there is the only way to put me to sleep."

"Put you to sleep?"

"Griffin says I get on his nerves sometimes. I guess all us AI's do. If we get too annoying he uses disks like that to house us. We each have our own unique disks."

The thought of multiple Ayla's didn't sound entirely bad. It was kind of freaky, though. Multiple AI with her level of functionality could take over the world if they really wanted to.

"So—there's more of you? More AI's, I mean," Chase said.

"Yup." Ayla nodded. "There's three more, each for the other members of your team."

"You keep saying it's going to be *my* team. Why?"

"The higher-ups." Ayla whirled around and her outfit changed to a business suit. "The people in charge think that you'll be best suited to lead for a bunch of different boring and complicated reasons."

"I have way too many questions." He flicked the disk. "So what would happen if I destroyed this? Would you cease to exist? Is that why I need to keep it safe?"

"Nah." Ayla twirled around and her clothes changed back into her casual outfit. "It's just so you can have some time away from me. I'm gonna live forever."

"Really?"

"Hell yeah." Ayla winked. "I can live inside of any of the electronics across the world."

Griffin burst back through the door. "Who's ready to become a super mercenary?"

Chase stood up. "I'm not *becoming* anything until you answer some of my questions."

"I think you'll be pleasantly surprised by what I have planned." Griffin waved for Chase to follow.

They walked through the doors and Chase stared at a room flooded with scientists waiting behind huge windows.

Every single one of them looked giddy to see Chase.

Each of them had a different gadget in hand, and Chase figured this was what Griffin meant by a quick tour full of demonstrations.

Chase scratched his head. "What am I looking at?"

"Ayla, would you be so kind as to assist our friends as we move from display to display?" Griffin asked.

Ayla spun around and her outfit changed to match the scientists behind the glass. "Sure thing, Griff."

"I let you get away with it once, but how many times do I need to tell you to stop calling me Griff?"

Ayla crossed her arms. "You don't tell me what to do. Not anymore." Her eyes fell on Chase with a smile.

Griffin sighed, "No, I guess I don't." Ayla warped into the first room and waved to them as Griffin began his speech, "As I said before, we want to amplify your heroics. If you agree to join the Interceptor program, you'll receive a set of gear, your own special weapon, the ability to control the element of your choosing, and of course, a special kit designed to amplify your strength and speed."

"That's a hell of a pitch."

"It's a hell of an *offer*."

"And what makes you think I wouldn't say yes just to get my hands on all the tech and then go do my own thing?"

"Because you've never cared about power, or money, or who needs saving. You do what you need to do." Griffin turned toward the room Ayla was waiting in. "Ayla, can you bring up a screen and play file fifty-two?"

She nodded and a video of Chase popped up on the glass. It was a kind of supercut of some of the misadventures he'd had throughout Sellea City with the Vanguard.

Chase wasn't impressed. "There's a whole group of people doing things like this."

Griffin wagged a finger. "But none like you, Chase. Come see."

Chase moved up to the window and watched as a scientist tried out a variety of gadgets.

"Tech for movement, defence, offence, and just about anything you can think of."

The scientist shot a couple of grappling hooks, formed and threw a shield that flew back to his wrist, and he made a shimmering barrier around himself. He finished up by sprinting around the room faster than Chase had ever seen a person run.

Even his own modified tech-cycle wouldn't have been able to keep up with speed like that. What Ayla was doing in the room wasn't clear, but it looked like whenever any of the tech was being used, she was focused.

"I'd get to use all that?" Chase asked.

Griffin nodded.

"Whenever I want?"

Griffin nodded again.

"All of that just to make protecting people easier?"

"Protecting people—and stopping Zeal."

Chase had a feeling that everything was going to be leading back to him. That sick mad scientist that created all those dumb bots. He had just appeared one day out of nowhere and unleashed hell.

As far as Chase knew, there wasn't a single person that knew who he was or where he came from.

"So, it's about him."

Griffin waved for Chase to follow him to the next window. "We have reason to believe that he's—getting more ambitious. There's only so much the police and the military can do against his creations. They're simple and dumb, but they aren't the easiest to wreck with traditional weapons."

"So this program is to create a team to beat that nut job into the past?"

"That's one way to put it. We'd rather erase him from history if you know what I mean."

Chase didn't entirely know what that meant.

"Like—like, kill him?"

Griffin looked confused. "Yes, Chase." He gestured to the next window where a scientist sat with a bunch of glowing cores. "This is a demonstration of some of the elements you can choose from. Same situation, your mastery of your chosen element allows you to do whatever you put your mind to, but you can only choose one for your kit—permanently."

"Do me and the others on the team have to pick different elements?"

"Not at all. I want you to pick whatever element calls out to you."

They watched as the scientist launched flames, ice, a green mist, light, shadow tendrils, and even more elements all from his hands.

What really caught Chase's attention was when the scientist slowed the blades of a fan to a near halt.

Somehow the facility had developed some way to slow specific objects down—like control over time itself.

The next thing that caught his eye was when the scientist controlled sand to come out of a bucket and it formed a big hand that waved to them. Once again, it looked like none of it would have been possible without whatever it was Ayla was doing in the background.

"How is any of this possible? I've never seen anything like this—even in the richer districts of the city."

Griffin laughed, "There are perks when you work for the government."

"That might be the shadiest thing I've heard all day."

The next series of rooms were filled with scientists hitting dummies with various weapons. There was every weapon someone could have thought of—swords, axes, bows, hammers, spears—if you could think of it, it was behind one of the panes of glass.

The two that stood out were a pair of what looked like gloves that sent a dummy flying from a light touch, and a short sword that morphed into a huge blade after the pull of a trigger. The issue was that the sword looked like a serious hassle to learn to use.

"See anything you like?" Griffin said as they made it to the last window. "You can always just use your knife if that's what you're most comfortable with."

"Yeah," Chase looked back at the gauntlets. "I guess you could say something caught my eye."

Behind the final window, there was a scientist in a high-tech black and gold suit. It looked like he could barely handle the weight of the material until Ayla flew right into the suit.

It was like the scientist sprung to life as he leaped around the room and tossed weights that had to weigh well over four hundred pounds as if they were nothing.

"So, you like what you see?"

Ayla flew back out into the room. "Pretty cool, huh?"

"This is—" Chase looked around again. "This is a lot. I just want to help people, I don't know if I want to be some kind of—wannabe superhero."

Griffin looked disappointed. "Don't think of it like that. Think of this as you being able to do what you already do, but with more ease—more safety and efficiency."

"Yeah, still—"

Griffin sighed and ran two fingers along the edge of his eyebrow, "Ayla, activate protocol twelve."

Ayla gave a concerned look. "Griffin—"

"Now."

Chapter 4:
A Messed Up Trick

Ayla nodded and after a moment, gas flooded into each of the rooms the scientists were in. They all tried to head for doors, but none of them were opening.

Whatever that gas was, it was choking them out.

Chase narrowed his eyes. "What are you doing?"

Griffin launched a fist toward him, but Chase ducked it. He caught Griffin's bright purple arm and flipped him to the ground.

After flipping up to his feet, he hit Chase with a kick. They circled each other, but Chase kept an eye on the gas-filled rooms.

"If you don't tell me what's going on——" Chase raised his fists. "I'm about to beat your ass, *Griff*."

"Don't call me Griff." He charged in with another wild swing, but Chase rocked him with an uppercut followed by a knee to the body.

Griffin dropped to the ground and something small fell from his pocket. There wasn't any time for that weirdo and whatever trinkets he had.

People were going to die.

Many of the scientists had already passed out—or worse.

"Ayla, can you do something?" She shook her head and hopped into the disk that he had pocketed. "Are you kidding me?" He looked around. "HELLO?! HELP! ANYONE?"

There was no answer.

Chase pulled his knife and jammed it into the nearest window, hoping it might shatter. The knife didn't even make it all the way through the thick glass.

"Gah! Stupid small knife!"

He looked around at the different panels outside each of the windows—maybe he could unlock the doors.

He fiddled with a few buttons, but nothing happened.

His eyes fell on the object that had fallen out of Griffin's pocket—it was a small keycard. He snatched it and rushed around the room trying it on the different panels.

A glass window finally slid open when he tried it on the room that housed the powerful gauntlets he'd wanted to try. The gas dissipated as the window opened, but the scientist in the room had vanished.

Chase set the gauntlets on his hands. "I really hope this works or I'm about to re-break my hand for nothing."

He moved to the next glass window and threw a heavy fist into it. Rather than shattering into a million pieces, it fell apart like it was made of blocks of stone.

Chase made his way throughout the room smashing the windows. With each one smashed, the gas in each room stopped pouring in. A bead of sweat dripped down his head as he smashed the last window.

As if prompted by a director, all the scientists stood up in unison. "Thank you for the assistance, Mr. Dyer."

Chase stared as the group of scientists calmly walked through each of their now unlocked doors.

"Okay, what the actual fu—"

Melodramatic clapping caught him by surprise.

He turned around and stared at a thrilled Griffin.

"You certainly do want to help people—you've made that abundantly clear, but I hope I've also made it clear that my tech can help you save even more lives."

"So, this was—"

Ayla appeared beside Chase. "A test, and as expected, you passed with flying colours."

"You guys are nuts! They all could have died."

Griffin waved a hand. "But they didn't because you saved them—with my tech. So, how would you like to join the program and lead the Interceptors?"

Griffin had to be some kind of mad scientist.

Putting someone through a life or death situation just to prove a point was insane, but at the same time, it was impressive that they had planned for just such an occasion. Whoever was in charge really had thought of everything.

Maybe joining wouldn't be such a bad thing for Chase.

The gauntlets were pretty cool after all.

"Is there any way I can think this over?" Chase looked at the gauntlets. "Maybe do some kind of trial period with some of the gear to see if it clicks?"

Ayla pouted, "Give him a bracelet, pleeeeeaaaa—"

"We can't afford it if he says no."

Chase held a hand out. "You have my word that if you let me take—whatever it is—as some kind of trial, you'll get it back if I decide this isn't for me."

"I can get in a lot of trouble for doing this." He buried his face in his hand. "Pick out your element, and weapon of choice. You can take those out on a test drive —two days—that's all you get to decide, and Ayla will remain by your side for that time. Understand?"

"Got it."

"I can't stress how bad things will get for you if you don't comply after the two days are up."

Griffin looked shaken.

He was speaking in such a hushed tone, it was like he was afraid that someone might be listening in to the conversation. He may have been a powerful man, but clearly, there was someone even higher up that struck fear in him.

Chase was going to have a serious decision to make, but he wasn't thinking about whether or not to accept Griffin's offer. He was thinking about whether or not to take all the tech right to the Vanguard.

If all of the tech was as good as Griffin made it out to be, it would probably be better in the people's hands instead of the hands of the government.

Ayla gave Chase a concerned look and he raised an eyebrow. "Everything alright?"

She nodded. "I think everything's going to be just fine. It'll be a fun two days."

She didn't seem as upbeat as she had before.

It was almost as if she could hear his thoughts.

Ayla's eyes nearly bugged out of her head.

Chase stared at her.

There was no way.

"Ayla, can you hear my thoughts?"

"You figured that out quicker than I expected." Griffin rubbed his head. "Yeah, she can hear all your thoughts, so long as you're in possession of that disk I gave you. If you join the program, the two of you will be neurally linked for the rest of your life."

Hi, Chase

He heard her voice in his head, but she hadn't moved her lips.

So, I can speak to you like this?

Ayla nodded. *You sure can.*

Chase shuddered, "I somehow feel incredibly violated."

"Go ahead and make whichever selections." Griffin clapped his hands "We'll get them ready and we'll have you sent back down to the city." Griffin looked at his watch. "I think you'll still be able to make that date."

Date?

Marin.

She wasn't going to believe what Chase had been through.

Chapter 5:
Marin, Meet Ayla

"Where is this lady?" Chase opened his visor to check the time—ten minutes past when they agreed to meet. "Must be runnin' on slums time."

He'd been able to bring the gauntlets he'd used in the facility for a little test. They'd given him a bracelet with a brown module set in it when he chose the earth element. Even cooler, Ayla had been able to reside within it.

The fancy suit or any of the other neat tech would have been even cooler, but he couldn't complain too much. He had a feeling that what he was in possession of was worth far more than anything he'd ever even been near.

You know if you synced your visor with hers again, I could tell you exactly where she is.

Chase jumped in fright at the sudden voice. "Maybe you should be out here with me if you want to talk to me." He checked down each side of the empty street. "It's all clear. I'm still not used to the whole—mind-speaking thing."

The bracelet glowed and Ayla hopped out. "Sorry. So, what's this Marin like? Is she pretty? Is she your girlfriend?"

"I thought you could hear my thoughts." He raised

an eyebrow. "Doesn't that mean you can read my mind?"

"No." She shook her head. "I can hear the thoughts you have. That's it for now."

"For now?"

"If you decide to join the team I'll have access to all of your thoughts and memories.

"Oh, goody." Chase started thinking of some of his embarrassing moments. "There's some early ammo for you."

"I won't make fun of you for any of that—much."

Marin stepped out of an alleyway just down the street. There wasn't a single person who'd have expected a girl like her to be a member of the Vanguard. She had a rather unique look, but she also looked like she should have been modelling for any reputable fashion company.

She waved, but her face and body language changed the instant she spotted Ayla.

"Uh—" Ayla rubbed her arm. "I've seen looks like that before. She's already jealous."

"Why would she be jealous?"

"Oh, you're one of those dense men. Look at me." She waved a hand down her body. "I'm hot."

Chase laughed, "Maybe a little full of yourself."

"Oh, shut up. I know you think so. I'm in your brain."

If Ayla was right, things could get a bit tense. Marin did have a bit of a jealous streak in her, something that wouldn't end well for her if she got on Ayla's bad side. If Ayla got made enough, she could probably disable all of Marin's tech.

"Chase, who's this?" Marin asked as she approached. "I've never seen her around before."

"This is Ayla." Chase flicked a thumb toward Ayla's toothy grin. "You're not going to believe what happened to me."

Marin gave him a confused look. "Yeah, I was a bit

confused when you shared your location with me and you weren't headed to jail—even more confused when you called me about dinner." She folded her arms. "Why *aren't* you in jail?"

"Hello to you too," Ayla cut in with an annoyed look.

She glanced at Ayla. "Feisty one you've picked out there."

"He didn't pick me out. I was designed for him."

Marin's face scrunched up. "What?"

Chase already knew that having to explain everything was going to be a pain in the ass. It was hard enough for him to believe, so a skeptic like Marin was probably just going to think it was all one big joke.

"This is going to sound super weird, but Ayla is an AI." Chase stepped in between the two. "An AI that this weird white-haired guy in a big bright suit made for me. He wants me to become a government-sponsored super mercenary."

Marin burst into laughter. "I needed that, thanks." She started down the street and wiggled a finger. "Come on. I'm hungry."

"Marin, I'm being serious." Chase rushed after her. "They want me to leave the Vanguard and everything. They gave me these gauntlets and this bracelet and—"

Marin grabbed his wrist and stared at the bracelet. "Always said you needed to learn to accessorize."

Chase felt his face get hot. Marin had a habit of not taking him serious in the moments when he was being most serious.

"Can you take this serious?" he asked. "I don't know what I'm going to do."

The night had grown dark, but the neon lights that danced across every inch of Sellea City almost made Chase forget about that fact. Everyone would always say how it felt like cities never slept, but in the case of Sellea

City, that was actually true.

Someone couldn't even be blamed for forgetting it was nighttime, because of how bright the lights, signs, and holos were.

Marin stopped and looked at Chase. "You're serious? You'd actually think about leaving the Vanguard?" Her eyes moved to Ayla who had been floating next to Chase rather than walking next to him. "She—is—floating."

Ayla looked at the ground. "Oh, yeah, I do that sometimes."

"How—are you doing that?"

Ayla shrunk down and perched on Chase's shoulder. "I can do a lot of things."

Marin pinched herself. "You aren't kidding." She circled them. "Ayla really is an AI—but—how is this possible?"

"Trust me," Chase scoffed. "I've been asking that pretty much all day."

"We're getting street-meat, then you're going to explain exactly what's going on."

Chase looked at Ayla and shrugged. "I'll do my best. Ayla, you think you could give us a little bit of privacy?"

She nodded and hopped back into the bracelet.

Marin stared at his wrist. "You have a girl living inside your bracelet. Now I've seen everything."

"You'd be surprised."

Marin led him a few blocks over to her favourite street vendor's cart. She nabbed a couple of burgers from him and they continued down the quiet streets. The entire way, Chase did his best to fill her in with the day's events, but it all sounded hard to believe—even after having experienced it all first hand.

"Okay, so this guy wants you for this special program. Do you think you're actually going to do it?"

Chase bit into his burger. "I dunno. It did feel pretty cool to smash all that glass with these gauntlets. I haven't even tried the element out yet—I'm not really sure how, if I'm being honest."

"The Vanguard has been your home for how many years?" Marin asked. "You're just going to up and abandon them? After everything we've all done?"

Marin assuming he'd just abandon the Vanguard without a second thought irritated him. "I didn't say I was just going to abandon them. I don't know—"

"Well, you're thinking about it. That means something."

"You didn't see what I saw. If you did, you'd be thinking about it too."

There was a moment of uncomfortable silence as they each finished their burgers. Chase was annoyed by the way Marin had reacted to everything. He figured his oldest friend would have been at least a bit excited to hear about the insanity he'd been swept up in.

They looked at each other, both prepared to speak, but no words were coming.

Chase opened his mouth, but Marin spoke first, "Even if you were to agree and take part in this program —what if we took the tech you had to the Vanguard?" Marin ran her hands along his gauntlets. "We could get them to scan the gauntlets, that bracelet—Ayla."

Before Chase could answer, Ayla appeared. "I'm going to have to go ahead and veto that decision. This is all top-secret tech. Griffin probably shouldn't have even let you take it for a spin—for this exact reason."

Chase raised an eyebrow. "What's the harm in letting our people scan this tech? We do what we do to help people."

"This tech is dangerous in the wrong hands." Ayla folded her arms. "I know you *think* the Vanguard always does the right thing, but—"

"Excuse me?" Marin said, clearly taking that a bit too personally.

"Don't get me wrong," Ayla stepped off the curb and looked around. "The Vanguard has done wonders. You all just—you don't know what Zeal is really like." She looked up at the moon. "If he found out a group like yours had this kind of tech, he'd wipe you all out in an instant."

"We can handle ourselves."

Ayla shook her head. "Not against him. Not the same way Chase and the rest of the candidates for—"

CRASH!

The sharp clashing of vehicles sounded like it had happened right behind Chase. They each looked around, but there wasn't any kind of wreck to be found. It had to have been right around the corner.

If there was any kind of time to test out the new tech, a sudden accident was going to be it.

Chase grinned at Ayla. "You got the location of that crash?"

She held up a finger. "Yup. Round the corner."

"Then let's go." Chase took off down the street.

Ayla flew beside him. "Griff told me that this is exactly the kind of person you are. I'm glad he was right."

"Help people, *and* play with the new toys?" Chase shrugged. "Sounds like a win-win to me."

Marin caught up. "Okay, but what are you expecting to do with super-mitts and a brown bracelet that you don't know how to use? It's a car accident, not exactly a Conk battleground."

"Aw." Chase smiled. "You called them Conks."

"For now." Marin rolled her eyes.

As they turned the corner the source of the crash came into view. It looked like one car T-boned the other. One vehicle had a crunched in front-end and the other was completely flipped over.

As far as Chase could tell, no one had been thrown from the vehicles.

For a second, Chase could have sworn there was someone up on a roof across the street, looking down at the scene from the shadows.

Marin looked around. "I'll call for an ambulance while you get to work."

Chase rushed toward the cars with Ayla. "Can you scan these and make sure the people inside are okay?"

"You bet I can." Ayla flew forward and inspected each vehicle. A green light washed over each of them as Chase arrived. "Driver and passenger in this car." Ayla gestured to the car with the crunched front-end. "Both with injuries a hospital will need to treat."

"Life-threatening?"

"No. Not if that ambulance doesn't come for another day or two."

"This other one?"

"One driver—surprisingly minor injuries, but he doesn't appear to be conscious."

Chase looked at his gauntlets. "Okay, so we just need to flip this bad boy back over." He rolled his arms. "I'll just give it a little love tap. That should be enough to flip it, right?"

"Chase, I don't think that's such a—"

He threw a slow, light uppercut into the car and it shot into the sky like a rocket.

If that driver really hadn't suffered any injuries, that was likely to have changed.

Chase's eyes bugged out of his head. "Whoops."

He stared at the car as it flipped and rolled in the air. If he didn't think of something fast, that driver was going to become one with his car in the worst way possible.

"I was trying to tell you it wasn't a good idea. Those gloves are going to register you not having a kit on as being at critical damage. Those things will hit anything you strike with the force of a bazooka."

He stared at Ayla. "You don't think this was VITAL INFORMATION to tell me BEFORE you let me down here to PLAY—AROUND."

Ayla pretended to scuff her foot along the ground. "It slipped my mind."

"Oh, good. How are we supposed to save this guy now?" Chase looked over to Marin who had her jaw wide open. "Great, we broke her too."

Ayla pointed to a transport truck that was covered with a tarp. "According to my sensors, that thing is filled with sand. If you use your earth element you can make a kind of dirt slide or something."

"That's convenient." Chase looked at the brown glow of his bracelet. "So, how the hell am I supposed to do that?"

Chase glanced up at the car again, but it looked like it was beginning the descent back down to earth. There wasn't much time.

"Well you *need* this to happen, right? You *need* to save that man?"

"Yes. I *need* to save that man *before* he becomes a *human-car smear*."

"Then make that sand do what you need it to. Tell it you need it to help you save that man. Will it to do what you need." Ayla said without a hint of concern on her face.

The situation was dire and she was asking him to do something he'd never in his life imagined was possible. Somehow, there didn't seem to be a single bit of data within her that didn't think he could do it.

The bright smile she had calmed him down.

He took a breath and held his hand toward the truck. "Okay, sand—I *need* you—"

Ayla grunted, "I didn't mean to literally ask it. In your head—focus and will it to move."

The car was plummeting toward the ground.

Something had to happen.

Chase focused his mind on the sand.

He focused on it flowing out of the truck, and after a moment, the bracelet on his wrist let out a strong glow.

The sand started to slip out of the truck.

Chase couldn't believe it.

It was working.

He pictured the sand turning into a hand and it did exactly that. The sand-hand flew up to the plummeting car and slowed its descent until it could stop it. The hand wrapped around the car and brought it back to the ground.

Chase had stopped a car that he had punched into the sky. He saved the day with a magic sand-hand.

What a weird day.

The sand fell away and Chase felt a serious ache in his arm. That ache washed along his whole body and it felt like he needed to spend a day in the hospital himself.

It was like everything he had just done was the equivalent of fighting an army of Conks by himself.

"I knew you could do it!" Ayla flew around him.

Chase tried to catch his breath, "I didn't—but I'm glad—I did. He all good?"

Ayla scanned the car again. "A few more injuries than before, but nothing that can't be fixed with a little bit of T-L-C."

Chase fell to his butt. He couldn't believe how drenched in sweat he'd become. The way his body ached, mixed with the cold he felt made him feel like he'd come down with some kind of flash-flu.

"Chase, are you okay?" Marin rushed over. "What the heck was that?"

He couldn't reply.

He was too focused on staying conscious.

Marin crouched down and put a hand on his shoulder. "What's going on?"

Ayla sat cross-legged in front of Chase. "His body isn't used to the toll of the tech. Right now, it probably feels like his body is on fire," She gave him a concerned look. "Am I right?" He nodded. "It'll pass soon. I promise."

"An ambulance is on the way, and that means cops too, we gotta get out of—"

Marin was cut short when Ayla shot to her feet. "Conks, incoming."

Chase tried to move, but his body wouldn't let him. Marin stared into the alley Ayla pointed toward. Two Conks with swords in the place where their hands would be stepped from the shadows.

That was new.

All the Conks Chase had ever seen only busted stuff up with their hands.

"They have swords now?" Marin asked.

Ayla looked down at Chase and held a hand out. "Chase's vitals still haven't returned to normal. Are you able to handle this, Marin?"

She looked nervous without a weapon. "I'm going to have to try."

The Conks charged with their swords at the ready as a figure hopped down from the rooftops. Chase recognized the black and gold suit in an instant. That was one of those suits from the facility, which meant whoever this guy was, he was a part of the program.

He pulled a staff from out of nowhere and twirled it around before taking a fighting stance. He parried the strikes from the Conks and battered them each to the ground.

He shoved the staff through one of the Conk's heads and sent himself into the air. With a quick turn of the staff dark green and purples spikes covered each of the Conks until they each detonated.

The man landed in front of Marin, but his eyes were on Chase. "They said you were supposed to be something special, but you're on your ass after using your tech once. Why the hell do they want *you* to be the leader?"

Marin stepped forward. "Who are you? One of those Interceptor dorks?"

The man smirked. "Something like that."

Ayla flew forward. "I'm certain Griff told you that all contact between potential candidates is forbidden. Leave, now."

"I just wanted to see why I wasn't picked as the leader. The kid can't even move—looks like someone made a mistake." The man jumped right back up to the rooftops and disappeared.

Chase staggered to his feet. "What—was that?"

Marin rushed over and threw his arm over her shoulder. "Come on. I'm taking you to the Vanguard for some rest. No arguments."

Ayla looked concerned. "Only to rest, right?" Chase reached into his pocket and pulled out Ayla's resting place. "Oh, don't you da—" Chase flicked the switch and Ayla flew into the disk.

"Let's go."

Chapter 6:
Welcome To The Vanguard

When they burst through the doors to the Vanguard headquarters, everyone rushed into action. Marin had called ahead and the group's top doctors were all ready and waiting. A couple of the newer recruits had gathered some light food and drinks as well. Chase knew he was an important member of the group, but he had no idea he was held in such high regard.

Marin held a hand up to the crowd. "He's okay." She helped Chase to a chair. "He perked up more and more the closer we got. I'm starting to think he was just being dramatic."

Chase rolled his eyes. "I've never felt anything like that before."

Marin looked at the group of people. "Everyone back to work. Someone go tell Tish we'll be coming to see her shortly." She pointed a finger at a mousey kid Chase had never seen before. "You, go tell Dante to get his tech booted up. We've got some things he might want to take a look at."

Everyone stared at Chase, who still looked like garbage.

Marin let out an annoyed growl, "NOW!"

Everyone scattered.

No one wanted to piss Marin off.

"Take it easy on 'em. Looked like there were some newbies in that bunch," Chase said as his lungs finally stopped hurting.

"I'd rather put some fear in their hearts early. Helps stave off the insubordination." She shot him an evil grin. "I wish I'd done the same with you."

"You love me too much."

"Whatever you want to tell yourself, mud-boy."

"Yeah," Chase rose from his chair. "We can squash that nickname right now—it was sand by the way, not mud."

"Sand-lad?"

There was time for Chase to come up with a totally-awesome and clever nickname later. Marin was never good at that kind of thing, so the sooner she quit with the —*endearing*—names, the better.

"Who's being insubordinate now?" He grabbed a bottle of water that was left behind and a suspiciously fresh peach.

Marin raised an eyebrow. "Are you forgetting who's the superior here?"

"I forget all the time when I'm the one wiping the floor with most of the Conks." Chase took a bite of the peach. "No big deal. Kinda so good at it that some shady secret government project scouted me." He held up the peach. "Where'd we get these bad boys?"

"Not even staying on topic—glad to see you're already feeling better." Marin headed for a set of double doors. "You might beat more—Conks—but I'm the one making the plans. Not sure about the peaches, though." She pushed the doors open and Chase followed. "Probably a new recruit from outside the city. I love it when they bring offerings."

The Vanguard Headquarters was a dingy little place, but it was home for Chase. The second-hand supplies and dull lighting gave it a covert feel, which fit as for the last few years being a member of the Vanguard had officially been deemed illegal.

That decision had only driven more people to become members. Every person in the Vanguard knew that they were helping the people of the city in ways that the government couldn't.

Chase looked down at the peach. "We aren't still forcing people to offer something when they join, are we? I told you guys that we needed to stop that sh—"

Marin cleared her throat. "I know you don't care about any kind of chain of command, but that doesn't mean it doesn't matter. You can leave the decisions to Tish and I."

He glared at the sudden outburst from his childhood friend. "I do leave the decisions to you guys, but you can't force people into some kind of fee to join. We're trying to help people, not rob them of their possessions."

"We do what we do in the interest of keeping the Vanguard strong." Marin stopped and put a hand on the door to Dante's workshop. "If people are able to provide food from their families farms, medicine, money—anything. It all helps."

Chase was interested in looking out for the Vanguard, but he couldn't get behind something like that.

He thought back to when he pitched sending out individual groups to neighbourhoods in strong support of the Vanguard. The idea that a group of people could go around collecting whatever donations people felt they could offer, was the better way to go.

"Whatever you say," Chase narrowed his eyes. "Madam Colonel."

She looked like she took offence, but swallowed her irritation as she entered the workshop. "Dante? You in here?"

Chase finished his peach and tossed what was left

into a trashcan as they walked in.

"Just finishing up," Dante called from under a desk. "What is it that you guys have for me this time?"

"You aren't going to believe any of this."

Dante's lab was one of the most impressive things Chase had seen—until he spent a day in a floating facility. Comparing the lab to the facility he had been in only a few hours ago was like comparing a zebra to the peach Chase had just eaten.

The rows of computers and cluttered desks gave the room more of a mad-scientist feel than it did a high-tech facility.

Dante shot up from under the desk. "Unless you guys are bringing me some crazy alien tech the world's never seen before, I doubt that."

"Set up a test dummy." Marin gave Chase an amused look. "I think we'll change your mind."

Dante looked confused, but he grabbed a small box from a drawer and tossed it to the floor. The walls of the box flipped open and a silver test dummy was constructed in its place. "Show me."

Marin gestured to the dummy. "Be our guest, sand-lad."

Dante perked up. "Ooh, trying out a new nickname?"

Chase glared at Dante. "We absolutely are not trying out a new nickname."

He adjusted the gauntlets on his hand as Ayla's words echoed in his mind. He needed to hit the dummy as carefully as possible.

He raised an arm and gave the dummy a slight nudge and it flew through the wall. "Crap. I really thought that would have been light enough."

Dante adjusted his glasses. "What the actual hell is on your hands?"

Marin cracked a smile. "We were hoping you could

give it a scan and tell us."

"Gladly."

Chase pulled Ayla's disk from his pocket. "I was wondering if you could give this a scan as well." He pulled his sleeve down to cover his bracelet as he handed the disk to Dante.

Everyone seemed a little too eager to get their hands on Griffin's tech. There wasn't any harm in not mentioning the bracelet.

Dante stared at the disk. "Typical data disk. What's so special about it?"

Marin laughed. "Just a little—"

"It's got some complex data I want you to take a look at," Chase cut in. "That's all. Maybe you can help me make some sense of it." He watched as Dante's finger neared the switch to wake Ayla. "DON'T—do not hit that little button under any circumstances."

Dante raised an eyebrow. "Why?"

"There could be—an explosion," he lied as he removed his gauntlets.

Chase couldn't help feeling guilty about lying to Dante. The two of them went way back, nearly as far back as he and Marin. Without Dante's brain, Chase would have been a goner years ago.

"An explosion of annoying." Marin rolled her eyes.

"It'll take some time for me to scan everything and make sense of the data." Dante took the gauntlets. "You guys want to hang around, or do you have something you need to do? Been a while since I've seen the two of you here, together."

Marin grabbed Chase's hand. "We've got to go have a little meeting with Tish, actually. Be done by the time we get back."

Dante nodded. "I'll see what I can do."

"That wasn't a request."

They walked out into the hall and Chase pulled his

hand free. "Do we really need to go see Tish? I'm still waiting for the day I see her and she doesn't immediately start screaming at me."

"Yes, we really need to see her. She'll want to know about all of this, especially if it means we might be losing you." She sounded hurt and annoyed all over again by the end of her sentence.

"I still haven't—"

"I know. You still haven't decided. That's part of the problem. Maybe Tish can help you decide."

They made their way down the hall to a crappy old elevator and Marin pushed the button for Tish's office. Chase always chuckled at how stupid it was for the boss to have their office on the top floor of any building.

Why couldn't Dante have had the top floor?

Whatever sciencey stuff he'd be working on had to be just as important as whatever it was Tish did up there.

Chase nudged Marin. "Think you can keep her from yelling at me?"

"Are you still on the yelling thing?"

He shrugged, "You know I hate getting yelled at."

"Oh," She grabbed his face. "I'll keep you safe, you big soft hero. Soft—like sand."

He pushed her hands away. "Quit it."

The mood in the elevator shifted and Marin looked at Chase with concerned eyes. "I was really worried back there. I don't think I've ever seen anything put you down for the count the way—whatever it was you did, just did. What was it like—doing that weird magic I mean."

The sudden concern caught him off guard. Marin wasn't exactly the kind of person who expressed their feelings everyday. Though, to be fair, Chase and Marin weren't the average person to one another.

"Hey," He placed a hand in hers. "I'm okay. It was weird. It was like I put every part of me out there. Like my soul flew out of my body and guided the sand to do what I wanted it to do. When I finished, it was like I had just got done a day-long workout—if that workout ended with me getting run over a few times."

"But the whole no talking thing and the sweating and the breathing—I just—it was—"

He squeezed her hand. "I'm fine. It's gotta be like a muscle. Ayla said my body just isn't used to it yet."

"Huh. Yet."

The elevator dinged and Marin pulled her hand back. The doors crawled open and the duo could already see Tish looking out to the city below. They made their way into the office, but Chase couldn't shake the conversation.

He hadn't even meant to, but he did say *yet*. Maybe somewhere deep in his mind, he'd already made his decision.

"We've got a problem, Tish."

Tish turned around and stared at Chase. "I'm not surprised. It seems like I only have the pleasure of meeting with Chase when something has gone horribly wrong." She gestured to two chairs. "What's going on?"

Chase ignored the offer of a seat and instead took a look around the office. It was strange that something so extravagant was *necessary* when the group was supposedly hurting for supplies and funds.

Marin took a seat. "Chase is thinking about leaving the Vanguard."

Tish's tone turned sharp. "What?"

He turned around. "Yeah, turns out I'm a pretty popular guy. Looks like I've got other options."

Marin groaned, "I can't keep her from yelling at you if you speak like that."

"So, what? Am I supposed to offer you something? Money? Higher rank? My undying appreciation?" Tish tapped her fingers on her desk. "You know how vital you are to this group, and you know what it may mean if you leave. Which leads me to the real question, *why* would you leave?"

If he really thought about it, there were lots of reasons as to why he'd leave. Nearly dying on every mission was at the top of that list, but it was also at the top of the list as to why he'd *never* want to leave.

"I'm about say this yet again, and even I still don't believe it." Chase started to fiddle with a set of pens on her desk. "Long story short, top-secret government project wants me to be some kind of government-sponsored hero."

"What does that have to do with the Vanguard?"

"They asked me to leave the Vanguard."

"Because you can't be a hero *and* be a member of the Vanguard?"

"Probably something along those lines," Chase shrugged. "If I had to guess, I'd say it's something to do with the branding."

"Just because we've been labeled as a threat to society, doesn't mean we actually are one. We do more good for the people of this city than—"

He held his hands up. "You don't gotta defend the group to me. I know how we operate."

Tish raised an eyebrow. "Then it shouldn't be anything to think about, should it? Yet it is." She snatched a pen from Chase. "You're having your doubts about my organization."

Chase stared at her. "Your organization? I thought the Vanguard is supposed to be the people's organization."

"Semantics."

"It's not semantics. I've been bringing my issues with the way the group is being run to the both of you, and you both ignore me every time."

"What do you want from me?"

Chase looked to Marin for help. Help that he knew

wasn't going to be coming. Over the last little while, her loyalties seem to have had drifted from him to Tish.

"I think what Chase is trying to say is that we've strayed a bit from what we were when we began. I just think—"

Tish gave an indifferent shrug. "If Chase is unhappy with the direction of the group he is welcome to leave."

She may not have been yelling at him, but what she was saying was somehow worse.

It pissed him off.

He'd done a lot of thinking about the success of the Vanguard, and anyone would be a fool to think that most of its positive image didn't stem from Chase.

Marin cocked her head. "Tish—"

"What? I have no interest in dealing with a headache that doesn't even want to be around. If you want to leave, so be it. There'll always be another Chase Dyer. Another young, headstrong, wannabe hero with a chip on his shoulder."

Chase stared at her. "That's how it's gonna be?"

"You aren't a boy anymore." Tish stood back up and looked out the window. "You can make your own decisions."

Chase looked from Marin to Tish. "I love this organization and what it stands for—I'm always going to. You, Tish—you're nothing but a soulless coward. I'm sure you'll be stepping into the field to make up for my absence, right?"

Tish was silent.

"That's what I thought."

He headed toward the elevator, but he could still hear Marin. "Do you have any idea what you've just done?"

Marin made it to the elevator as Chase pushed the button to get back to Dante's workshop. "Chase, she's just hurt. You've done so much and she—"

"I'm not interested in excuses. If she really is hurt and overreacting, she knows how to contact me. In the meantime, I'm going to go see how I can help people—rather than taking their things."

The ride back down to Dante's workshop was a quiet one. Partially because Marin didn't know what to say, and partially because Chase had nothing else to say.

He was ready to pack up his things and leave, whether Dante was done with his scans or not.

Chase stormed into his workshop. "Dante—finished yet, or what?"

"Gauntlets are all done." He adjusted his glasses. "Some crazy tech there. Most complex tech I'd seen until the scan on this disk started. Maybe one day I'll be able to make some weapons that can match those gauntlets, but who knows how long that'll take."

Chase put the gauntlets back on. "The disk?"

"I'm about halfway through it now. There seems to be two sets of data on there—highly complex as well, but even more so than the gauntlets. It appears to be two separate AI programs."

"Two?"

Dante nodded. "One named Ayla, and one named Alyx. I just finished the scan on Alyx, the system is preparing for the scan of Ayla."

"Alyx? You know what? Nevermind. Abort the process. I'm getting out of here."

"But it'll only be—"

Marin sighed, "Dante, do as he asks, please."

Dante started typing at one of the consoles and a chamber that the disk was floating in popped open. The disk dropped to the bottom of the chamber and he took it out.

"I don't know how you got this, or who made it, but all of this is way out of our league. The kind of data and functionality in those gauntlets and that disk alone are like—a hundred years off." Dante handed the disk to Chase. "Be careful with all this."

"I'm getting it out of here, aren't I?"

Dante gave him a confused look and Marin stepped forward. "Tish basically just told Chase to take a hike."

Dante's eyes went wide. "Screw her."

Chase smiled. "Glad someone's on my side." He pocketed the disk and headed toward the door.

"Chase," He turned and looked at Dante. "If you ever need anything—forget the Vanguard—you know how to reach me."

"I'll see you soon, Dante," Chase said as he headed out toward the entrance to the building.

Marin was right on his heels again. "I feel like I need to say something."

Chase stopped. "Then say something."

He could tell his brief turn had caught her off guard. Marin was looking for anything to say to keep him from going. Unfortunately for Chase, he was hoping for something that he knew probably wasn't ever going to come.

"What if I don't want you to go?" she finally asked.

Chase scoffed, "Does that really matter at this point? What Tish says goes. Just because I'm not a part of the Vanguard doesn't mean we're not—whatever it is we seem to be doing. I can still see you anytime."

She looked like she was fighting back tears. "You don't know that. The Vanguard are nothing but a bunch of problematic criminals to the government, and—and you'll just be another one of them. How do you know you won't have to arrest me on-sight the next time you see me?"

"Marin," Chase took her face in his hand. "When have I ever—and I mean *ever*—given a solitary shit about any rules at all?"

She laughed, but her expression shifted to anger and

sadness. "Don't walk out that door, please."

"Goodbye, Marin."

Chase pulled the disk out of his pocket and hit the switch as he walked out into the street.

Ayla popped out and stretched. "Well, now I feel violated, so I'm going to assume you didn't listen to me."

"Ayla—"

"And next time I'm speaking," She folded her arms. "I'd appreciate it if you don't cut me off while I'm in the middle of being sassy."

"Ayla—"

She started to pace back and forth. "Being sassy is always the best part of my day, and even an AI needs to enjoy the little things in life. Got it?"

"Are you done?"

"Yes."

"Good." Chase looked up toward where the facility was hidden. "I'm ready to accept Griffin's offer."

Chapter 7:
What's A Team Without A Leader?

Chase walked through the doors of the floating facility once again. Rather than annoyed confusion, he felt a sense of calm. There was no telling if leaving the Vanguard was the right decision, but somehow he knew that joining the Interceptor program was the right one.

There was a tiny part of him that wished he could have brought Marin along, though.

"Alright, Ayla, where are we supposed to be headed?" Chase looked around at the ludicrous amount of doors leading out of the central room. "You guys really need to get a receptionist or something."

She giggled, "You don't need a receptionist when you have an AI."

"So everyone in here has one?"

"No, just you and all the other soon-to-be Interceptors."

"Then how does anyone else get around here?"

"Secret government facilities shouldn't be the easiest things to get around in." Ayla started toward a door and waved for him to follow. "I'm sure everyone that works on something here knows exactly where they're supposed to be, and they only head to where it is that they're supposed to be."

She had a point. It's a lot harder for people to sneak

out with secrets if they have no idea where the best-kept secrets are. If they let Chase leave the facility with Ayla, they probably had even wilder stuff tucked away even deeper inside.

"I still have some questions about why anyone would build a facility in the sky rather than underground, but I figure you're just going to brush it off."

Ayla shrugged. "There's time for all of that later. Today is supposed to be a fun and happy day. You're officially becoming the leader of the team!" Ayla shrunk down and perched on his shoulder as Chase entered a hall.

"Can you at least tell me about Alyx or that weird guy from last night?"

"Alyx? Who's Alyx?"

What an interesting development.

What's an interesting development?

Chase groaned, "I need to stop forgetting you can hear my thoughts." He turned a corner and Ayla pointed to a door at the end of the hall. "What about that guy with the staff?"

"Well," Ayla brought a finger to her chin. "It makes more sense if you just meet him yourself."

Chase approached the door and it slid open. "Yeah, but he didn't exactly seem—thrilled about how I handled the situation last night."

"He'll warm up to you." Ayla gave him a side-eye. "Takes a little while, but I have a feeling that most people do eventually."

"Ha-ha."

Chase made his way around rows of computers to where Griffin was looking out a huge window. The window looked down into a separate room where the sounds of fighting and explosions could be heard.

He looked down at what looked like a perfect recreation of the shopping square he'd fought the Conks in when he first met Griffin. What was different was the three people rushing around in black and gold suits.

Griffin turned around with a toothy grin. "You have no idea how happy I was to get the news from Ayla." He shook Chase's hand. His icy hands surprised Chase. "We're so excited to have you in the program."

Chase pointed to the action below. "So that's the rest of the team?"

Griffin nodded. "Kyrie, Sable, and Dorian. You'll meet them all soon." He headed for another door. "First, we need to get you kitted up. Have fun with the toys?"

"Oh, yeah." Chase rubbed the back of his neck. "You probably should have let me know about the whole bazooka on my hand thing. Kinda took me by surprise at the worst possible moment."

Griffin chuckled. "I saw the play-back—but I also saw what you managed to do with your element, and on your first try no less."

Chase raised an eyebrow. "So what I did was impressive?"

"Absolutely! The others already have a week or two on you in terms of training, but none of them managed to get their elements working on the first day of training."

"Told you." Ayla tried to nudge him. "You're a real hero."

The next room was separated into four sections. Three of which were stripped bare of their contents, aside from a few bare mannequins. The fourth section had everything Chase had seen the scientists playing around with during his first visit.

He stared at the black and gold suit. "Can I try the suit on?"

"We call it a kit. Your kit to be specific." Griffin put his hand on the mannequin. "It's been imprinted with your DNA, meaning you're the only person in the world that has access to this here kit. If you want to put it on, just put your hand on it. The kit will handle the rest."

"I'm gonna ignore my thousand questions about the DNA thing, but that sounds simple enough."

"Well," Griffin shook his head. "It's a bit more complex than just that. You need to brace yourself once you've claimed the suit."

It was like every time Ayla or Griffin explained one thing, a thousand new questions came right along with whatever new concept they introduced. Super-suits sounded simple enough. Needing to brace for a suit just made it sound like it chafed in all the wrong places.

"Brace myself? What for?" Chase asked.

"The suit is imprinted with your DNA so it has to run a check through your body to make sure you are the correct host. You're going to feel a kind of intense shock for a couple moments. Try to clench and tense your body or you may end up—"

Chase cocked his head. "End up what? Dead?"

Ayla giggled. "You might poop yourself."

"What?"

"The shock can cause your body to let some *stuff* loose. We found that out the hard way, huh Griff?"

Chase thought back to the three badasses fighting an army of Conks. "So one of them out there—one of them crapped their pants?"

Griffin nodded. "Yes, but no I will not tell you who it was."

Ayla had a mischievous grin plastered on her face. "I might."

Chase stalked toward the kit.

If something like that was going to give him the strength to leap to the tops of buildings, that was something he wanted constant access to.

He put a hand on it, and the material crept from the mannequin and down Chase's hand. Somehow, it slid inside the bracelet on his wrist.

Griffin wasn't kidding about the kit handling things. There was a bit of tingling, but not really any intense shock.

"That's it? That wasn't so—"

A jolt of electricity rushed across his body. He could feel his body twitching all over.

To put it mildly, the shock sucked.

Once it faded away, he looked down at his hands. "Intense shock. Got it."

"We all good—" Griffin raised an eyebrow. "Down there?"

"Shorts are clean. Maybe you guys should iron the kinks out of that. That frickin' sucked." He ran his fingers across the bracelet. "Just wondering, what would have happened if it *didn't* find my DNA as a match?"

Griffin looked uncomfortable. "The shock would have continued until you were dead."

"Oh, fun." He stared at the bracelet. "What do I do now?"

"I'll be helping you with that part." Ayla returned to her normal size and held a finger to his face. "It's similar to how you made the sand do what you wanted. You need to force the kit out—you need to will it out."

More of the willing. Chase wasn't even sure how he made a sand-hand, and now he needed to coax a suit with stage freight to come out.

Griffin nodded. "But first we need to do the not-so-fun part."

Chase raised an eyebrow. "That is? I thought the shock would have been the not-so-fun part."

"The neural link. More of an issue for Ayla than it is for you."

Chase wasn't sure what it would feel like to be permanently linked to an AI, but he figured anything attaching itself to your brain can't feel the best.

He was in a constant state of a thousand questions.

Would it hurt?

Would he have access to all the information Ayla had access to?

Would he start seeing the world around him in a series of green numbers?

"Relax, Chase. It'll just take a sec." She flew into the bracelet and it started to glow once more.

He could feel a strange sensation wash over his body. After a few seconds, it felt like someone had hit a switch in his brain that put all of his senses into overdrive.

Ayla flew back out and smiled at him. "Well, what do you know? We're officially partners for life now."

Chase smirked. "Till death do we part."

She shrugged. "Something like that."

"So that's it? That didn't seem so bad."

Griffin looked at his watch. "Three, two—"

Ayla brought her hands to her head. "Here come all your memories." She dropped to the ground and groaned in pain.

Seeing a program in pain was a strange feeling. She looked like she was just an ordinary woman having the most intense migraine possible. What was it about memories that caused an AI pain? Was it the sheer volume of memories and experiences or some other weird side effect of merging together?

Ayla stumbled back to her feet and looked into Chase's eyes. *Link successful.*

Weird.

Right?

"What exactly was it that was causing you all that pain?"

"It was feeling every single one of your experiences. Every moment of your life all cramped into a few seconds. All your happiness, pain, and anger. It's a lot."

"Whoa."

Griffin laughed. "Whoa is right. Ayla did a good job. One of the other AI's had to boot down to restore full functionality after that. It seems our black and gold kits do much better with the process than the newer models —interesting—"

"Looks like Griffin's in his own world. We can put the kit on, right?" Chase asked.

Ayla nodded. "Focus on getting it to cover your body. I can help."

He closed his eyes and did what he could to coax the kit to cover his body, but it didn't feel like anything was happening. He popped an eye open and the sleek black and gold kit had covered his body. Whatever material the kit was made from, Chase couldn't even feel it on his body.

"Congratulations, you're officially an Interceptor. The leader of the Interceptors." Griffin looked impressed. "You're a natural."

"That was way easier than the sand."

"That's because of yours truly." Ayla spun around. "The element stuff should start being a lot easier now too!"

Griffin pointed at a door in the corner of the room. "Head through there and you can meet your team. After that, I'll get you set up so you can test out the kit."

Chase nodded and Ayla flew back into Chase's bracelet. He made his way through the sleek white corridors until he came to a large set of elevator doors. They slid open as he approached and after he stepped inside it started moving without him touching any buttons.

"Ayla? Are you doing all this?"

I am pretty much all-powerful in this facility, but no. We've just got some neat tech.

That's for sure.

The elevators came to a stop and the doors slid

open. He saw a huge empty room with the three team members standing around. Somehow the room must have been able to project a perfect copy of Sellea City.

The most impressive thing was thinking back to the explosions—there was debris flying everywhere, so everything that this room had constructed was somehow interactive.

Any tips for meeting everyone?

You already know Kyrie doesn't like you. Just try to get on his good side, and make nice with the twins.

Twins?

Chase started toward the group and the one woman amongst them waved. "You must be our fearless leader. It's Chase, right?"

The closer he got the prettier she became. She looked like someone had made her in a lab to be most people's idea of an *ideal* woman. Her sleek yet curvy figure was something to behold, but Chase couldn't help wondering if it made fighting a bit more of a challenge.

Then he remembered Ayla was hearing every single one of those thoughts and he buried them.

"You got it." He nodded. "They've been kind of tight-lipped about all of you guys. Clearly, I'm the most in the dark here."

The woman's twin stepped forward. "Griffin seems to be like that. That name's Dorian." He gestured to the woman. "This is my sister, Sable." He pointed at the man Chase had seen the other night. "That ray of sunshine over there is Kyrie."

Dorian looked ready to win every and any weightlifting competition across the globe. A guy like that could have dominated anyone he came across.

While Kyrie had a smaller frame than the beast of a man that Dorian was, he still looked like he could hold his own in a fight with little problem.

Chase looked around at the boring room. "You guys

been training long?"

"Two weeks in my case." Kyrie narrowed his eyes. "You'd think the man who's supposed to lead this team would have been the first to sign up, not the last." He shrugged. "You'd also think that the man who's supposed to lead our team wouldn't be a kid."

"Starting with the tough guy act right away, huh?"

Kyrie got in his face. "It's not an act."

"What's your deal, dude?" Chase created some distance between them. "Sorry if your life was kind of mundane before all of this, but I had a lot going on. Needed some time to think."

"You're exactly what I expected. I give them a week before they name me the team leader instead."

Chase shrugged. "Glad you think so, but I don't suddenly stop being more awesome at random." He smirked. "You're fighting an uphill battle, buddy."

Sable stepped in between the two of them. "Alright, alright. Good to know who the hotheads are here." She looked at Dorian. "Looks like we get to be the voice of reason for once in our lives." She turned her attention back to Chase with a smile. "I'm looking forward to working with you."

Chase shook her hand. "I'm looking forward to it too. I'm kinda used to dealing with Conks by myself, so having a super-duper crew'll make things a breeze."

Dorian jutted his head toward the elevator. "Let's give Chase the room so he can practice with his kit. I want a front-row seat to see what he can do."

One by one they all made their way out of the room and back up to the overlooking room. They were—an interesting group, but Chase had worked with worse in the Vanguard.

"Aw, crap. I didn't even get to ask them about their gear or their AI's."

You're a team. There'll be lots of time for that later.

"Fair point."

A voice came over a loudspeaker, "Why don't we get you started with some quick solo training? You ready, Chase?"

Chase looked up to the window and flashed a thumb. "Let's do it."

A blue glow washed over the room and a rundown section of Sellea City was constructed around him. He took note of the dirt patches and figured those were for him to try using his element. Chase recognized the street he was on, it was Apple Street in the heart of the slums.

A group of Conks appeared but remained motionless.

"Ayla, can you go ahead and take Chase through his kit's gear?" Griffin asked through the loudspeaker. "Once he's had a try of everything, we'll allow him to play around."

Ayla nodded and she cycled through each of the different types of tech he had at his disposal.

Just like the scientists had shown, he could access shields and grappling hooks on each arm, an energy shield for full-body coverage, and boosters in the legs of the kit.

Every piece of tech had its benefits and its downfalls. Something as complex as the energy shield ate through the kit's power, while the smaller shields barely made a dent.

"Your suit only has so much energy." Ayla watched as Chase threw and caught a shield. "It will naturally recharge over time when not in use. The more energy you use, the less of your kit you'll have access to. Using your element will eat at your kit's power supply. The same goes for damage—get beat up too much, your kit will need to recharge."

"Don't use too much power, and don't get my head

caved in. Sounds simple enough." He looked up to the window. "I think I'm good to start."

Another blue glow washed over the room, and the Conks sprang to life. Ayla merged back into the bracelet as Chase examined the various Conk's movements.

He was surrounded, but he wasn't worried.

The kit made him feel stronger than he ever could have hoped to be, and his gauntlets gave him a storm of confidence.

"Alright, Ayla. Let's beat some bots."

Please don't tell me that's going to be your catchphrase.

"Well—not anymore."

Thank god.

Chase rolled his eyes and rushed toward the nearest Conk. He concentrated on having the earth under its feet swallow it, and sure enough, the Conk's feet sunk. He launched a fist right into its head and it sparked as it flew through the air.

"I can punch you bastards now," Chase said with a mischievous chuckle.

He readied himself as a wave rushed toward him, but everything faded away before they reached him. He was glad the suit felt natural to use, but that was barely any kind of practice.

The loudspeaker piped up again, "Chase, get back up here. We've got a problem, which means it's time for the team's first mission."

Chapter 8:
The First Mission

Jumping out of a plane was going to be one hell of a way to start the first mission. The whole thing seemed a bit simpler than Chase was hoping for, but simple was probably for the best considering a team he'd never worked with was involved.

Griffin gave the team a proud look. "Remember, the four of you are tasked with locating and protecting a pair of scientists. The building could be crawling with Conks —Chase's name for Zeal's bots—so extreme caution should be exercised."

Griffin seemed nervous as he briefed the team about the vital information of the operation, but that wasn't true for everyone. It wasn't Chase's first time taking the lead on an operation, so he was confident he could remain in control.

The others on the team looked just as collected as Chase felt.

"The Yorks. Husband and wife." Chase adjusted his gauntlets. "Lab is on the third floor, but at this point, they could be anywhere."

Griffin smiled. "That's why you're the leader."

Kyrie rolled his eyes. "We all knew all of that."

Chase sighed, "Dorian, you and Kyrie can start from the top down. Sable and I will start from the bottom and work our way up." He moved toward the opening. "We all regroup on whoever finds the Yorks first, understood?" Everyone nodded. "Then everyone get ready. It's almost time to jump out of a plane—with no parachutes."

Kyrie bumped Chase. "If we come across any other civilians we need to make sure their safety is prioritized. The Yorks can wait."

Chase rose an eyebrow. "You aren't the one calling the shots here. The Yorks are priority number one. We'll keep everyone safe, but they come before everyone else."

Kyrie got in his face. "There isn't one person who comes before any other."

Kyrie was the type to run headfirst into every situation with his emotions flaring. Chase was on a pretty good role of making sure no one died on his watch. Sure, people got hurt on the odd occasion, but that was practically unavoidable.

"I'm not saying that." Chase pushed him back. "Our mission is to protect and extract the Yorks specifically. We'll keep everyone else safe while we do that, and that'll just a cherry on top of the operation." He looked out to the city below. "I have no issue fighting for as long as we have to to keep anyone else safe once we've gotten the Yorks out, but they're first. If they're our target, that means they are someone else's."

"That's *if* anyone else is even there." Dorian elbowed Kyrie. "Sounds like the team lead's got you beat on this one."

Chase smirked. "Alright. We'll jump on three. One— two—" Dorian and Sable jumped out of the plane. Chase sighed as Kyrie shrugged and did the same. "Three." Chase rolled his eyes and hopped out of the plane.

The drop was higher than the ones he was used to off of skyscrapers, but he didn't feel an ounce of fear. It's like the kit made him confident in his ability to land safely on the ground—parachute or not.

Ayla appeared beside him complete with goggles and a wingsuit. "Sky diving is kinda fun."

"AI can have fun?" Chase asked.

Ayla scrunched her face. "You need to stop asking things like that. Of course I can! I can get awfully annoyed by you, can't I? Why wouldn't I be able to have fun?"

"Huh," He chuckled to himself. "I guess I didn't think about it that way."

As they reached the top of the city, the way the sun peeked from behind the buildings almost helped calm him down. The sun was setting on the horizon which made the view on the way down even more beautiful.

Even though Ayla was just an AI, her presence made it feel like he was watching the sunset with any other real person.

She clicked her tongue. "Just an AI?"

Chase brought a hand to his face. "One of these days I'm going to remember you've got twenty-four-seven access to my brain." He looked down at the building below. "Ready on the shield?"

"You bet."

Chase watched Dorian and Kyrie land on the roof of the building as Sable landed on the ground outside. As he rushed past the roof he could have sworn he caught Kyrie flipping him off.

There was no telling if Chase would ever warm up to that asshole.

He nodded at Ayla and she activated his energy shield right before they collided with the ground. The shield absorbed the impact, and Chase landed on the ground as if he had only taken a small hop.

"That's never going to not be cool."

Sable put a hand on his shoulder. "Nice landing.

Ready to beat some ass?"

"Ready to beat some ass?"

She shrugged. "Felt like the right thing to say."

"I don't know what type of training they have in mind for all of us, but I think we could all definitely use some one-liner training."

"Cleverness isn't my strong suit—" Sable unsheathed a sleek black and gold katana. "But I make up for it with my blade."

"Then let's beat some ass." He turned his attention to Ayla. "You ready?"

"Always."

Sable smiled. "Hey, Merikh." Her AI jumped from a necklace and hovered next to her. "Can you go ahead and gimme a scan of the building? Any immediate threats or small clusters of people?"

Merikh was different from Ayla. He didn't look like he could blend in with a crowd of people due to a blue hue that covered his image.

He nodded and a yellow flash shot through the building. "It seems as if most of the inhabitants have managed to flee the building. There appears to be two groups of two people that Zeal's forces are converging on. Floors five and seven. A man with a young girl, and a woman with a young boy."

Chase cocked his head. "Do you think the Yorks could have brought their kids into the building with them?"

Sable gave him a confused look. "I don't know why they would, but I guess it can't be out of the realm of possibility. At least we know where we need to go."

Sable and Chase rushed inside the building and each of their AI flew back into their accessories. If the other two were smart enough to do a scan of the building as well, both groups would have two protectors each. They'd all be able to converge and get them out.

"Ayla, stairs?" Chase asked as he and Sable looked around the dark building.

A wave of energy washed over the building again.

End of the hall on your left. It zig-zags every floor. Up a set, back down the hall, and repeat.

"Got it. Let's go," Chase said to Sable as he rushed down the hall.

They were shocked at how few Conks there were to fight. The odd Conk would jump out to slow them down, but it was nothing a quick punch, or slash of Sable's sword couldn't handle.

It was a good thing the kits increased their stamina because Chase was pretty sure he'd be covered in sweat if he had to climb five stories without it.

When they made it to the fifth floor they didn't need their AI to scan in order to find their targets. The horde of Conks attempting to break through a heavy metal door was all the information they needed.

Sable lifted her sword. "Hang back and wreck any of them that I miss."

Chase nodded and Sable shot forward.

She was using the thrusters in her kit, but she was also creating flames as she pulled her sword down and scraped it across the ground. The flames grew to the ceiling as she slashed her way through the Conks in one mighty swing.

That was pretty—hot.

Really, Ayla?

I know you were thinking it too.

I was groaning about your pun.

The Conks Sable had missed were torched by the flames of her element. Chase rushed in and landed a couple of quick strikes on each of the Conks to break them into pieces.

He turned his attention to Sable, who hadn't moved from a crouched position since her attack. "You alright?"

She stood up slowly. "Yeah. That just——" she said through heavy breaths. "That just takes a lot out of me, but it was worth it."

Chase cracked a smile. "Can't argue with you there." He turned his attention back to the door with a few solid bangs. "It's all clear out here! Is that the Yorks in there? We're here to provide you guys with some evac'."

After a moment and some rustling, the door slid open and they were met with an older man and his young daughter. "I'm Cassian—Cassian York." He gestured to the terrified girl. "This is my daughter Lenna."

Chase clued in to the fact that Griffin hadn't shown them pictures of the Yorks, but as soon as he spotted Cassian's name tag, he knew they'd found the right man.

Lenna hugged into her father's leg. "Daddy, who are these people?"

"It's alright, sweetheart." His eyes flicked from Sable to Chase. "Who exactly are you people? How did you know we needed help?"

Those were good questions. Griffin did a great job briefing the team on the details of the mission, but he didn't do a great job of letting them know what to say to the Yorks.

Sable crouched down and smiled at Lenna. "We're the good guys." Lenna wasn't sure what to make of Sable, but she managed to calm her down a bit.

"We're new to all of this," Chase said as he scanned the hallway for more Conks. "But you can call us Interceptors. I'm Chase, and this is Sable. The government sent us in here to protect you and your family. Is there anyone else——"

Cassian's eyes nearly bugged out of his head. "My wife—my son. We got separated, they're somewhere——"

Chase held up a hand. "There's two more of us and they started from the top." Some kind of commotion echoed through the halls from above. "Odds are—that's our team saving them right now."

Sable stood up and looked down the hall. "We'll take you two to them and then we'll get all of you out of here together, okay?"

Cassian stepped out of the room between Chase and Sable with his daughter in hand. They kept the Yorks in between the two of them in case of any surprise attacks. Wherever the attack came from, the other could easily speed over and help keep the scientist and his daughter safe.

"Feel free to tell me to screw off if it's none of my business, but what is it Zeal and his Conks are after here?" Chase called toward Cassian. "I assume you have some idea of what they want?"

Cassian nodded. "A program. My wife and I just had a breakthrough on a program we're working on."

Sable looked back. "What kind of program?"

"The kind of program that would, unfortunately, be of great interest to a madman like Zeal. It allows for the dissemination of medical supplies on a continental scale at roughly medium efficacy."

"Why would Zeal be interested in something like that."

"If effective medicines could be aerosolized en masse to tend to wounded warriors in times of conflict, that means other things could be aerosolized as well."

"With some kinda screwed up poison—" Chase's eyes went wide. "Zeal could wipe out an entire continent without lifting a finger. Where's the lab where you've been working on this?"

"It's where I left my wife—"

"At least we know why we had it so easy now." Sable's eyes snapped to Chase's. "We need to pick up the pace."

They rushed up to the next floor and spotted Kyrie

and Dorian as they finished the last of their Conks. They had to deal with far more, but it wasn't anything they had a problem with.

Dorian waved. "Looks like you guys beat us to the punch. We'll have to buy you guys dinner or something."

Kyrie narrowed his eyes at Chase. "How do we even know those are the Yorks?"

Kyrie's questioning of Chase's every move was getting really old, really fast.

Chase shrugged. "Because he told us—and that name badge he's wearing with the photo of Cassian York looks an awful lot like him."

"Relax, Kyrie." Sable sheathed her sword. "We had a horde of bot's—"

"Conks," Chase cut in.

"Horde of Conks—to deal with too. Not our fault we did it better." She held up a hand and Chase high-fived it.

Kyrie banged on the heavy metal door. "Mrs. York? We're here to help you. We've got your husband and daughter out here as well."

"Cass? Lenna?" A female voice called through the door.

"Mommy!" Lenna cried as she rushed to the door.

"It's us Lyra," Cassian moved toward the door. "Please tell me you and Rhys are alright."

The door swung open and Lyra stood there with Rhys grasping onto her leg. "He's okay. We're both okay."

The united family embraced and Chase couldn't help thinking back to his own family.

It was moments like that, that he missed the most.

"Not to ruin the moment or anything," Chase said as he approached Cassian. "But we need to get all of you out of here before things get too hairy. Is there any way we can offload your program data onto a disk, or a server, or something techy like that?"

Lyra gave Cassian a concerned look. "Why does he know about the program?"

"I told them. We can trust them." Cassian put a hand on her shoulder. "How many people do you know that can take down more than one of Zeal's robots without any help?"

Chase waved a hand. "We're calling them Conks now. Trynna to get that name to stick."

"Conks," Cassian said with a nod.

Chase was loving how quickly everyone was adopting the knew name for the robots. At that rate, all of Sellea City was going to be calling them Conks by the end of the week.

Lyra looked at the team. "If we had some kind of secure network—someplace safe, we could just upload everything to that. Then we wouldn't need to worry about Zeal attacking a centralized location."

Chase perked up, "I think we actually have just the thing. Ayla?" She flew out of his bracelet. "Were you listening to everything?"

"I have no choice," She spun around and her outfit morphed into a scientist get-up again. "But I think I know what you're saying. You want me to route all the program data to the facility? We can keep it safe there until someone decides what to do with it."

Chase turned back to the scientists who each stared at Ayla. "That sound good to you guys?"

"You are aware," Lyra pointed at Ayla. "That girl just jumped out of your bracelet, right?"

"It's a long story," Dorian cut in. "We need an answer, now. What's it going to be?"

Cassian nodded. "If it's the safest thing to do, then let's do it."

Ayla smiled as she headed into the room. "Don't worry, the facility I'll send the program to, it's with the government too. That's how we know you guys sounded the alarm for the building."

Sable turned to Chase. "You've got a defence plan here, fearless leader? I have a feeling we haven't seen the last of the Conks today."

A defence plan wasn't in the briefing, so it was time to improvise. The issue with improvising was that Chase had no clue what each member's strengths and weaknesses were.

"Why don't you and Dorian keep an eye on things out here, while Kyrie and I keep an eye on things in the lab?" Chase turned to Kyrie. "Or is that going to be a problem?"

Kyrie shrugged. "Just lets me show you exactly why I oughtta be the leader."

Chase rolled his eyes. "Whatever, dude." He looked at Dorian and Sable. "That work for you two?"

They nodded and posted up by the door while Chase and Kyrie headed into the room with the York family. Ayla had disappeared, but due to the neural link, Chase knew she was inside the computer at the end of the room.

How long is this going to take?

It's a complex system. Maybe—five minutes.

Anything we can do to make things go—

A tug at his pant leg caught his attention.

It was the young boy, Rhys.

"What's going on buddy?" Chase crouched down. "Everything cool?"

"I like your suits."

Chase smiled. "Thanks."

He looked down at the boy's ragged shoes. It was clear that the family wasn't living the life of luxury as his shoes had bits of duct tape holding them together. Despite their dull appearance, the sneakers still lit up with each of the boys steps.

"I like those cool shoes you've got on. Did you pick those out yourself?"

Rhys nodded.

"You've got better style than me, kid."

Rhys looked around "What happened to that pretty girl? I thought she came in here."

"Ayla?" He shot a thumb toward the computer. "She's in that computer right now."

"In the computer?" The kid's face lit up. "That's awesome."

He laughed. "It is pretty awesome." Chase looked over at Rhys's happy family. "You must be a pretty brave guy."

Rhys scratched his head. "I didn't do anything."

"Didn't do anything?" Chase whirled his head around in an over-the-top manner. "What!? I saw you making sure your mom was safe!" He poked Rhys's chest. "That makes you a hero in my books."

"Really?"

"Sure does, buddy. Biggest one I know."

Rhys ran over toward his mother. "Mommy! Did you hear that? He said I'm a hero!"

Chase was always forced into acting like a big brother to the younger members of the Vanguard, whether he liked it or not. It was moments like that one that reminded him why he didn't mind taking up that role.

"I did." Lyra smiled. "You are a hero. You're my little hero." She picked Rhys up as some kind of commotion started outside.

Kyrie brought two fingers to his temple. "Sable, Dorian, we good out there?"

"We've got some kind of movement, but our scans aren't picking anything up," Dorian called back.

The sudden slash of a blade sent Dorian rushing across the doorway and a brawl started outside the room.

CRASH!

Debris shot to the floor as the lights in the room sparked. A person floated down through the hole he'd blasted in the ceiling—a person Chase had only ever seen from a distance.

It was Zeal.

The twisted psychopath in the flesh.

He let out a horrifying cackle as he stared at the terrified York family.

"Look at the little—what was it? Oh, yes. Interceptors." He almost seemed amused by Chase's surprised look. "Secret projects don't remain secret when you're infinitely powerful, boy." He stared at the computer at the end of the room. "Ayla my dear, exit the computer now—or I will kill everyone in this room."

Kyrie rushed at Zeal.

Without him even breaking his line of sight, Zeal held a hand up and a block of ice slammed into him, sending him sprawling to the ground. It looked like the impact of being squished between the block and the wall had knocked him out before he even hit the floor.

Before Chase started to move, a wall of fire surrounded him. "We don't need you rushing to your death just yet, now do we?"

"Not gonna lie Zeal, I already knew you were an asshole, but you're even more of an asshole in person."

His eyes twitched as he stared at Chase. "Chase Dyer. You were a pain before you were an Interceptor, and you'll be a pain long after, I'm sure."

Chase looked over at the family—it looked like the parents were saying their goodbyes already.

Some faith they had in the Interceptors.

The two kids stayed put as the scientists ran toward the computer at the end of the room.

Chase needed to keep Zeal's attention.

"You don't know me." He tossed a book at Zeal, but it disintegrated before it got anywhere close to him. "I try to not socialize with people who look like they cut their own hair."

"You're an insolent fool, and you will die that way."

Chase shrugged. "Sounds like a cool way to go. Better than a psycho with really bad eyebrows."

"Get out of here, NOW!" Cassian shouted at Zeal.

"Or what?" Zeal let out an amused chuckle. "I'll either be taking your program, the two of you, your children, or all of the above. It's your pick. Maybe I'll take the boy regardless, it would be interesting to see what may happen—"

"If you don't leave now, we'll take our thumbs off these consoles, and the entire room will blow. You'll get nothing and you'll be dead."

Zeal looked down his nose at them. "You're bluffing."

"Try us."

There was a scary pause in the room.

Kyrie was still on the floor, but at least the kids were inching their way toward the door.

Their parents must have told them to sneak out.

Zeal was considering his options.

How close are we?

I'm just about done. A few more seconds.

Whatever it means to hurry up, do that.

Zeal shot toward the scientists.

BOOM!

Everything was a blur.

All Chase could hear was ringing.

He wasn't able to protect himself properly without Ayla's help, and now he wasn't even sure if she still existed. His entire body hurt the same way it had the first night he used his earth element. His heart was pounding, but it wasn't because of the pain, it was out of concern for everyone else that was caught in the blast.

I'm still with you Chase.

Good. Everyone else?

Ayla?

No.

The room was filled with smoke, debris, and fire. The lack of any human sounds was what worried him most. He could see Kyrie stirring, but he expected him to have survived the blast if he had. Sable and Dorian must have rushed in when they heard the blast because Sable helped him to his feet.

Zeal was nowhere to be found.

Neither was Cassian nor Lyra.

The Transfer?

I managed to complete it.

Chase found Rhys laying on the ground. He was still alive, but he looked like he'd taken a serious blow to the head. When they found Lenna, she was in even worse shape. She'd taken some kind of serious impact to the head as well, but something had hit her arm during the blast. Sable nearly threw up as she did what she could to patch up the girl.

The mission was a failure—
But they weren't going to let those kids die.

Chapter 9
Those Poor Kids

"I did what I could, but she's losing a lot of blood. We need to get her to a hospital." Sable brought a hand to Lenna's forehead.

Chase stared down at where her arm used to be.

He wondered what their life was like before any of that had happened. It couldn't have been the worst life with two important scientists for parents, but now things were going to seriously change.

If she even made it.

No.

Chase knew he couldn't think like that.

He still hadn't fully recovered from the blast, but he knew something needed to be done. "Dorian, Sable, are you guys able to carry them?" He looked at Kyrie. "I don't know about him, but I'd rather let someone who didn't explode carry the kids—just in case."

Kyrie nodded. "I'm not gonna argue there."

The room was lit only by a red emergency light. It gave the room an ominous feeling, but it was probably a blessing that kept them from seeing just how blood soaked the room actually was.

Chase was never particularly squeamish, but being in a room where people had just died was a totally new feeling.

Dorian hoisted Rhys over his shoulder as Sable carefully lifted Lenna.

Dorian flashed a thumb. "Leave them to us." He turned toward the door. "Pandora, where's the nearest hospital?"

Dorian's AI, similar to Sables—but with a purple glow, appeared in front of him. "Just a few blocks over. Not far at all."

Sable headed for the door. "We'll rush ahead and stay with the kids until you guys show up."

They each disappeared into the building and Chase looked over at Kyrie. "Not a great start, huh?"

Kyrie narrowed his eyes. "Everything was going fine until that asshole showed up. What happened back there?"

Chase waved him over. "I'll tell you on the way."

Something about the run to the hospital felt off.

He knew the kids were going to be alright—on some level. Chase just couldn't shake a strange feeling. That wasn't going to be the last time they'd see that psycho, even if it seemed like he blew up along with the York parents.

Chase and Kyrie caught back up with the twins and after getting the kids checked in, the others had decided to head back up to the facility.

Chase needed to wait and make sure the kids were at least conscious before he left them on their own. It was his group's failure that led to their hospitalization.

To the loss of the poor girl's arm.

To the loss of their parents.

Their lives had changed forever and not at all for the better. Two more kids that had to live long, hard lives without their parents.

"You really should see if the doctors will take a look at you. I can see how your body is doing, and—"

Chase shook his head. "I'm not doing anything until

those kids wake up."

Ayla gave him a concerned look. "You can't blame yourself."

"Who else can I blame? It was our job to protect Cass and Lyra—to protect their kids." Chase was surprised when he spotted Griffin coming down the hall. "What are you doing here?"

"The others told me you'd likely still be here." Griffin looked through the window to the kid's room. "They filled me in on the details of the mission."

"What are the odds we're all getting screamed at by some government stooge tomorrow?"

Griffin didn't meet his eyes. "Let's forget about that for now."

Chase knew that meant he was absolutely going to be screamed at by a government stooge. Someone dodging answers was never good for anyone looking for answers.

Chase looked in at Rhys. "What happens now? Zeal wasn't only interested in their parents. For whatever reason, he was interested in the kids too, specifically the boy, Rhys."

"What? Seriously?"

"I was as surprised as you were. I don't know if he meant it as some sort of bargaining chip or something else, but he threatened to take the kids."

Griffin nodded toward the doctor. "Have they been updating you at all?"

"Yeah. They said that with the head trauma they suffered—from the explosion—they're not likely to remember much of the event—if they even remember any of it. It's possible the event itself will come back to them eventually, but the minor details of who was there and why everyone was there might just be gone. They may never even know that the team was there."

"That's useful," Griffin said as he brought a hand to

his chin.

"How dare you say that about them." Ayla looked like she wanted to punch Griffin as hard as she could. "Useful that those poor children won't be able to remember the horrible day when they lost their parents? When that poor girl lost her arm?"

Even when Ayla had her tense moments, she always had a hint of humour behind the things she said or the things she did. At that moment, Ayla was entirely serious. It was sweet to see how much she cared.

A computer program was sweet.

Weird.

"That's not what I—at least they won't have to live with that memory, Ayla," Griffin snapped at her. "I meant that it's useful because it makes them easier to hide. I can make sure they're placed in a group home in the slums. It won't be easy for them, but they'll be safe. We'll make sure to have someone keep an eye on them and check in from time to time. As long as we keep things quiet, Zeal shouldn't ever be able to find them."

Chase raised a finger. "I'd like to volunteer for that. I don't want to try to be a big brother or a dad—I just want to be able to make sure they're getting by." He balled his fists. "Being able to drop in that little bit of luck when things aren't going their way for a bit too long. Would that be okay?"

Ayla actually had a tear streaming down her cheek. It wasn't real, but it could have fooled anyone.

"Yeah. I think that would be best," Griffin took a shaky breath. "Poor kids. I'll make the arrangements and then scrub the data from everything. The only people who'll know where the kids are will be you and Ayla."

Chase raised an eyebrow. "You mean *you*, me, and Ayla?"

Griffin almost looked upset by that comment. "Yes— of course. Misspeaking."

Ayla perked up a bit. "The mission wasn't a complete failure."

"What do you mean?"

"Before everything went down, I was able to transfer just about ninety-nine percent of the program data to a secure server up in the facility. If someone wants to yell at the team for letting innocent people die, so be it. They can't be yelled at for letting that data fall into Zeal's hands."

She had a point, but it was still a hollow victory in Chase's mind. People had died on his watch, and that was never going to be something that would sit right with a guy like him.

"This is good." Griffin shook a finger. "I might actually be able to save all of our asses after all. If we have that data, that's a victory. We lost two good scientists, but they did what they had to to keep Zeal from snagging that data."

Chase looked at Griffin. "You guys know what he wanted that data for don't you?"

Griffin adjusted his suit jacket. "Would you like to come back to the facility with me, or are you planning on coming back on your own?"

Another. Damn. Deflection.

He started to walk away when Chase didn't answer.

After a few steps, Chase grabbed him and slammed him against the wall. "I'm done with you keeping me in the dark. If you want this to be a team, you're the one that needs to start acting like it. The York's gave us some idea, but I want to hear it from you—why does Zeal want that data?"

Griffin sighed. "We have reason to believe he's preparing for a hard reset of the world."

Chase let him go. "So—what? He really wants to wipe out humanity?"

He shook his head. "Not just humanity. Technology.

He wants to send us back to the stone-age. We just aren't entirely sure how he plans to do it yet. We had our suspicions that Zeal would have an interest in that program, and today confirmed it."

Chase looked back at Lenna and Rhys in their beds. "Just go. I'm going to hang around until they're done floating in and out of consciousness."

Griffin nodded and headed back where he had come from. He was a strange young man, but he had a good heart. It would have been easy for the average government drone to just forget about the kids, but Griffin putting a plan in place to keep them safe told Chase he'd made the right decision.

He just wished Griffin would finally trust him and start giving him the full truth in every situation from the start.

Chase smiled at Ayla, almost wishing he could put his hand in hers for some level of comfort. Instead, he rested his hand on the edge of the window sill.

It looked like the young girl was stirring, but she was clearly in a lot of pain. It was a hard scene to look in on.

Chase looked at his hand, Ayla had laid her hand on top of his in such a way that it looked like they were holding hands. It wasn't quite the same as a human touch, but it was just as good.

Just as meaningful.

"Thanks, Ayla."

She kept her eyes trained on Rhys. "We're partners. That means always being there for each other, no matter what." She perked up a bit as the young boy started to stir. "Looks like it's time for us to get back to the facility."

Chase groaned, "I hate—"

"You hate getting yelled at," Ayla giggled. "Tomorrow is gonna suck."

"Yup," he sighed. "Tomorrow is gonna suck."

Chapter 10:
A Weird Place For A Fight

The team didn't just get yelled at—they were punished. Despite Griffin's best efforts, a collection of other bright suit clad men admonished the team for their failure without acknowledging the small victory with the data. They made it abundantly clear that if the team screwed up again, the project would be scrapped.

To ensure the higher-ups knew what was going on at all times, they were planning to set up an initiative to record and broadcast the teams exploits to the public.

It would be like a stupid reality show, but instead of relationship drama, it would be real people struggling to keep the world safe.

The team piled into the enormous training room along with Griffin. Everyone looked disappointed or irritated in their own ways.

Chase had a feeling that there wasn't anything the four of them could have done against Zeal. They may have powerful tech behind them, but they hadn't had much time to train with it alone or even together as a team.

Griffin spoke first, "Don't take anything they said personally. They didn't say it, but they're grateful that you managed to at least keep the program data from Zeal."

Kyrie raised an eyebrow. "Don't you think our first mission being a complete failure is exactly why we need to reevaluate the composition of this team?"

"Really?" Chase rolled his eyes. "If you want to be leader so bad, go right ahead. I did my best to call the shots back there and I think we were all doing pretty good until Zeal got the drop on us." He narrowed his eyes at Kyrie. "Let's not forget who it was that got one-shotted by Zeal."

Kyrie scoffed, "I'd like to see you take a hit like that and then see how much of a big man you are." He turned his attention to Sable and Dorian. "And you two —what was even going on out there? Couldn't pick anything up on a scan, but you guys started fighting something."

The twins were annoyed with Kyrie. Anyone could have seen that. All of his words had a habit of striking and burrowing under people's skin.

Dorian got in his face. "You need to check your ego. If we weren't posted up at the door, there's no telling what might have happened."

Chase cocked his head. "What do you mean?"

"There were Conks that we'd never seen before." Sable tapped her fingers on the hilt of her katana. "They were cloaked—they blended in with the walls. We were all alone one moment, and then we were completely surrounded the next moment."

Dorian was still staring at Kyrie. "I barely managed to dodge the first strike."

Kyrie pushed him back. "Big bad Interceptors afraid of a couple basic bots?"

"They weren't basic. These were intricate. They didn't fight like any Conk I'd ever seen," Sable snapped. "I doubt you would have done much better, considering an ice cube did you in."

The tension in the air was palpable.

Kyrie didn't have a single issue with coming across like a bad guy. Everyone was annoyed, but they were getting the most frustrated with him.

Griffin held his hands up. "Alright, we need to take some time to cool—"

"We're here now." Kyrie gestured around the room. "Why don't we do some real training and see who actually is the best? Who should lead this team, and who should sit back and keep their mouths shut."

Griffin brought a hand to his brow. "Chase wasn't picked as the leader based purely on skill or strength. There was a lot that went into that decision."

Dorian cracked his knuckles. "I'm game to show you I'm better than you. People might actually listen if I was the leader."

Kyrie shrugged. "That's two of us."

Chase looked at his gauntlets. "Honestly, punching you in the face sounds like fun right now. I could blow off a little steam."

"This macho energy is pathetic." Sable drew her katana. "If it'll make everyone happy, I have no issue being the leader."

"There's no point in doing this!" Griffin bolted into the middle of the near-brawl. "What do you think you're going to accomplish here? You're supposed to be a team! You aren't supposed to be fighting over who should be the leader."

Kyrie let his kit cover his body. "Teams need to get past their disagreements. Knocked out, give up, or lose your kit—you're out."

Everyone nodded as their kits slipped across their bodies.

Chase wasn't usually quick to jump to violence against people, but it felt necessary. All Kyrie had done at every step was undermine and disrespect him. Maybe if he could show him how good he really was, he'd be able to bring the team together.

"You need to stop this—"

"Shut up already. This is happening," Sable snapped at Griffin. "Go set up a simulation that's fair for everyone."

Griffin trudged back up to the overlooking room. Everyone readied their weapons as Griffin started to type.

This isn't a good idea, Chase.

What am I supposed to do? It's not like this was my idea. Besides, everyone wants to do this.

We could talk to them and maybe—

What's that going to do at this point? Why don't you just stay out of this until it's done?

The room morphed into something rather surprising —a children's playground. It was a large playground with a surrounding forest to make up much of the other space.

In a way, it did make sense.

There was earth for Chase, and open space and things to ignite for Sable's fire. He figured that the intricate design of the playground would prove useful for Kyrie's poison in some way thanks to those spikes he could launch from his staff.

What about Dorian?

Chase had no idea what element or even what weapon he had. By the time they caught back up with them in the building, Dorian had already put whatever weapon he was using away.

"Do what you must," Griffin said over the loudspeaker.

Chase looked at the others. "Any other rules?"

Kyrie rushed at Dorian with his staff.

"I guess that's a no."

As Kyrie approached, Dorian grabbed his belt and a

sinister scythe formed in his hand. Kyrie barely had the time to deflect the strike. They clashed, and the resident nuisance backed off as he whirled his staff over his head.

Dorian looked over at Chase and laughed. It was kind of weird to turn his attention to Chase, but Dorian was a bit of a weird guy.

—

Something was wrong.

Weird. I—I can't move. Ayla?

Staying out of it.

Ugh.

No matter how hard he tried, Chase couldn't move his body. He was frozen in place, and he was thankful when Sable rushed to join in on the fight instead of attacking him. It was strange—maybe the explosion had damaged his kit somehow.

There wasn't any time to figure out the problem.

Time.

Dorian's laugh.

Chase remembered the blades of that fan from Griffin's demonstration.

Dorian was using the time element.

He must have been laughing because he was keeping Chase frozen in time. It was a useful skill, but it looked like it had its downsides. Dorian was almost entirely stationary as well—he only moved enough to deflect and dodge Kyrie.

It looked like he wasn't having the easiest time keeping Chase still either. He took a slash and Chase stepped forward, but when Dorian glanced over he was frozen again.

Dorian backed away from the fight as Sable kept Kyrie busy. The two balanced on top of a set of monkey bars as they duelled.

It seemed like of the entire group, Sable had the best grasp on using her element. Every strike she made featured a wave of flame that had to be causing small burns on Kyrie and his kit.

"What's the matter? Our fearless leader too afraid to move?" Kyrie asked as he broke free from Sable. He rushed toward Chase with his staff at the ready. "I'm not going to let you just hang back while the rest of us fight."

As Kyrie got close enough to strike, Sable caught Dorian with a slash.

Chase could move.

The staff came toward Chase's head and he deflected the strike with his forearm. He launched a heavy shot toward Kyrie, but he slid out of the way. Chase followed up with a kick that was enhanced by the thrusters on his leg and he caught Kyrie hard across the face. Kyrie flew through the playground and up a slide.

Chase brought his hand to his brow. "And—he's—outta there!"

Kyrie wasn't the one they needed to focus on, though.

It was Dorian.

He may not have been as good with his element as Sable, but his was even more dangerous. Chase had two serious issues—he needed to get his kit's power down to get the best use of his gauntlets, and then he needed to be able to get in close to Dorian.

Chase used Sable's pressure on Dorian as a way to push into the mix. He launched a few quick strikes at each of them, but they managed to back away.

Dorian landed on a roundabout as Chase approached. With a quick kick from Chase, the whole thing started spinning at top speed. He ducked a slash from Dorian's scythe before a kick sent him onto the roundabout as well.

After two quick rotations, Chase had already had enough. "Sorry about this, Dorian. This sucks."

"Yeah—you're a dick," Dorian looked like he was

ready to vomit. "But it was a good move."

Sable hopped onto the equipment and Chase ducked another slash. The three of them started trading slashes and blows as they spun around. Every time Chase dodged an attack, he got scratched by the other twin's weapon.

The entire roundabout shot into the air, and Chase spotted Kyrie back on the ground. He must have used his staff, the kit's strength, and the leverage he had to launch everyone into the air.

Dorian flipped to the ground first, ready to put Kyrie in the ground. He stalked toward him and nailed him with a whirling slash and a huge kick.

He had to have hit him pretty hard because almost the entirety of Kyrie's kit had left his body. All that remained was some light protection for his chest.

Sable rushed at Dorian again, and Chase followed on her heels. She slid between his legs and let a deep slash run across a leg. Flames exploded from beneath him and his kit dwindled down as the flames flared.

Chase flipped over Dorian, and as he looked up, he threw a heavy strike into his face—once again sending Chase into the air. He was in a bad spot, but at least Dorian was down for the count.

"Dorian's done," Griffin said over the loudspeaker. "Do not attack him."

Chase tried to control his spin as he fell to the ground, but on the way down, Sable launched a few fireballs his way. The only way he wasn't getting a face full of fire was to get his element working again.

The force had thrown him over a large sandpit and he held his hand toward it—begging it to protect him.

As the flames reached him, blocks of sand rushed up and took the force of the fire. Rather than just blasting the sand away, the fire was so hot that it actually turned the cubes into crude glass. Chase kicked as many as he could toward Sable as he hit the ground hard.

She slashed her way through the glass and smirked at Chase. Sable dragged her sword along the ground and a wall of flame rose into the air.

It rushed toward him and it only got more imposing the closer it got. The fire wasn't even near yet, and he could already feel what was only a fraction of the full force of the heat. Luckily, Chase still had the advantage.

He looked down at the sandpit and focused on creating a door. The wall of fire met the door as Chase took cover. It once again super-heated the sand into glass, but it was enough for Chase to barrel through. He crashed through the glass but fell short when he reached out for an attack.

When he looked up, Sable held her sword to his throat. "Looks like I win—"

A sudden flurry of staff strikes crashed across Sable's body and her kit was disappearing fast. She'd already used a lot of power using her element, but the powerful poisoned strikes from Kyrie were taking an even bigger toll.

As Chase scrambled to his feet he could see black and purple rashes forming all over her body, and she dropped to the ground.

"Kyrie, that's it. Sable is done," Griffin warned.

Kyrie smirked at Chase. "Let's go then, cap."

Chase tried to raise his fists, but only one arm moved. He looked down at his other arm—the one he used to block Kyrie's first strike against him. It had the same purple-black rash that Sable had.

Kyrie must have poisoned him right from the start.

Chase smirked right back at him. "You know you're only going to look like an even bigger idiot when you lose to me while I only use one arm."

Kyrie laughed. "You match the little girl now."

That struck a nerve.

Chase clenched his good fist. "I'm gonna put you through the wall."

It was down to the two of them.

It was time for one last attack.

Chase boosted forward and Kyrie did the same.

All he would have to do is touch him with one of his gauntlets, and he could have launched Kyrie right out of the room. He kept his eyes on Kyrie's staff as he twirled it. He was able to avoid telegraphing where his strike was coming from or where it was going to land.

Griffin teleported into the room between the two and held a hand out toward each of them. A flash went off and everything went white.

Chase dropped to the ground and rolled to a stop, and it sounded like Kyrie had done the same.

"THAT IS ENOUGH." Chase couldn't see Griffin, but he could hear the hurt in his voice. "You are supposed to be a team. If this is how you're all going to act, maybe you shouldn't be a team."

Chase rubbed his eyes as he rose to his feet. "I'm sick of this. Gimme a call when you figure things out. I'll be doing my own thing in the city until then."

Chase shot Kyrie a glare as he stormed past him. Dorian and Sable looked almost ashamed of what had happened, but they didn't speak up. He shoved the doors open and left them all behind.

Chase?

What do you want?

Why don't we go get a burger?

Do you really think that's going to change anything?

I can see you're hungry. It can't hurt to have a bite and think things through. No one likes a hangry boy.

Chase didn't want to admit it, but she was right. Something to eat would be good.

Ayla giggled. *I know I'm right. I'm me.*
Oh my god.

Chapter 11:
Ayla The Love-Bot

There's nothing worse than realizing someone else was right, all because you were hangry.

Chase finished the last bite of his burger and sighed. "What're we gonna do, Ayla?"

Chase was seated on the edge of a building overlooking the city, and Ayla leaned her elbows against it. "Seems to me like all of you need to quit with the dick-measuring contests."

Chase was surprised by the vulgar nature of her comment. Ayla exuded the kind of energy that few people do, that make it shocking to hear them curse.

She puffed her cheeks and blew out the air. "Who's leading and who's better shouldn't matter. The point of the Interceptor program is to protect the people of the city from things the police and even the military can't handle."

"I know, I know. It's mostly Kyrie. He just keeps getting under my skin."

She raised an eyebrow. "Maybe that's why he thinks you shouldn't be the leader."

"It's not like he'd do much better." Chase shrugged and chucked his crumpled burger wrapper.

She laughed. "In the field, no. I don't think he's the right choice. Maybe one day, but not now." Ayla looked up at him. "Maybe everyone needs to take a step back. All of you are the kind of person that hates to lose. Some time apart to clear your heads will do you good."

"Maybe."

Chase wondered if it would have been better to stick with the Vanguard after all.

Jacking the tech and using it to further the Vanguards mission might have been the better thing to do. They wanted the same thing as the Interceptors, they were just doing it in their own way. A more organized and honest way—even if Chase didn't agree with all of their decisions.

Ayla flew in front of him, breaking his train of thought. "I haven't had the chance to ask you yet, how would you like me to look and sound?"

He cocked his head. "I'm sorry—what?"

She twirled and her clothes changed into a more glam-rock look. "Well, you've seen me do my changey-thingy—I can look however you want me to." Her voice shifted into a strange accent, "Ah ken ev'n soond annay wey ah wont."

Chase had seen his fair share of bizarre things around Sellea City. As one of the last major cities on the planet, Sellea had its fair share of weirdos. Still, nothing he'd ever seen topped Ayla.

"Let's just stick with your normal voice."

Her accent dropped, "Sounds good to me. I like the Sellea City accent anyway. What about how I look? Do you want me to look like someone? A famous model? That famous lady you have those weird dreams about sometimes?"

Chase rolled his eyes. "You don't need to do that."

She spun and became the perfect copy of Marin. "I could look like her if you wanted. I can feel how much she means to you."

It felt wrong looking at an AI copying the image of

Marin, but he wasn't sure why.

"Why don't you just make yourself look however *you* want?"

"Really?" She twirled back to her usual look and brought a finger to her chin. "Are you sure?"

Chase shrugged. "Who am I to tell you what you should look like? You're your own person. We're—friends. Still feels kinda strange to talk like this to an AI."

She crossed her arms. "I'm more alive than those weirdos who subjugate themselves to a nine-to-five that they hate every day."

She had a point.

Ayla was as human as any other person someone could pass on the street. She may not have been able to touch people, but being able to control most electronics made up for that. In a place like Sellea City, Ayla had more power than any ordinary person.

"I guess, could I make one tiny request—on your appearance?"

"Shoot—and it better not be creepy or you better believe I'm going to find a way to smack you."

"No, it's not creepy," Chase said with a laugh. "I was just wondering if you'd be willing to give yourself green eyes."

"Green eyes?"

"I thought you experienced everything I have. You should know why I'm asking."

Ayla shook her head. "I have access to all of that, but I would never go through your memories without a good reason. They're your memories."

Chase smiled. "Well, at least that makes the whole neural link a bit less creepy." He watched as her eyes shifted from a stormy blue to a soft green. "Green eyes suit you."

"Why green eyes?"

Chase looked away. "My brother had green eyes."

"We've never talked about your family."

"That's because I don't talk about them too often."

There weren't too many people in Sellea City who knew a single thing about Chase's family. As far as he knew, only Marin knew anything of any real substance, while people like Tish knew tiny bits of information here and there. The topic was rather taboo.

Ayla shrunk down and stood where Chase was looking. "What happened to them?"

He sighed and looked off toward the city. "They're all gone." His eyes fixated on a few cars driving around the streets below. "My little brother's name was Run—"

Ayla's face scrunched. "Your parents named their kids Chase and Run?"

"If you think I'm weird, just think about how weird my folks must have been." Chase gave a half-hearted laugh. "We were out playing in a section of the city we weren't supposed to. Long story short, he stepped out into the road as a car came flying through."

Ayla covered her mouth. "I'm so sorry."

"I was the big brother. It was my job to protect him, and I failed." He could feel his emotions welling up, but he didn't want to give in. "After that, my parents never forgave me. They wouldn't admit it, but I knew. The way they glared at me every time they saw me—"

There was a moment of silence before Ayla spoke, "What about your parents?"

Chase shrugged. "Dad got sick and passed away while I was still in the academy, and shortly after that, my mum decided it wasn't worth it to stick around just for me." He took a deep breath, "That's when I joined up with the Vanguard and well, you know the rest."

"Where does Marin fit into all of that? Did you meet her through the Vanguard?"

He shook his head. "We've known each other pretty much since we were born. Marin's family practically raised me after my mum was gone."

"But you like her?"

Chase felt his face get hot. "I never said that."

"Well she likes you, and it seems like there are some pretty spicy memories here in the filing cabinet of your mind that I could access."

He was thankful Ayla was able to pick and choose what memories to access. She didn't need to dive into the world of Chase's complicated relationships.

"It's a long story."

"So—that means you two—? You know…"

"I can't tell if you're trying to find out about my love life or if you're just an AI that loves to hear gossip."

She shrugged. "Little of A—little of B. Why don't you give her a call? I bet talking things through with her would help more than they would with me." She shook a fist at the sky. "One of these days you'll love me as much as her."

Ayla was already great at pulling him from his bad moods. "It's a competition now?"

Ayla scoffed. "Of course not. I don't want to dust her that bad." She winked. "I just mean we're still new friends. We'll grow on each other."

"I've tried sending her a few messages, but she hasn't responded. I think it kind of hurt her when I left the Vanguard."

It was rare for Marin to stay mad at him for longer than a week, but while she was mad, she was *really* mad. She would become hurricane Marin, and no one wanted to get in the way of her wrath.

A devilish grin scrawled across Ayla's face. "I could *make* her answer your call."

"I don't think that would make anything better."

"Well, how about—"

"If I call her will you stop?"

"Literally immediately."

Chase sighed and opened his visor.

He didn't have to do much scrolling considering she was the only person he ever called. He selected her number and the call started to connect. The odds of her answering his call were slim, so he was surprised when she did answer.

"Chase?"

"Marin."

"What do you want?"

Ayla made a face like she wanted to comment on how bad that question sounded. Marin was still hurt about the whole situation with the Vanguard.

"I wanted to see you. Could we talk?"

"Uh—" It sounded like there were some other people in the background. "Sure, as long as it's quick. I gotta go, but if you want, I'll send you an address in a sec. You can meet me there in fifteen."

"Got it."

The call disconnected and after a few moments the address popped up. Marin didn't exactly sound like she was interested in seeing him, but he was willing to take what he could get.

It felt like it had been a long time already.

He missed his best friend.

"Did I tell you it would go well, or did I tell you it would go well?" Ayla said with a smug look on her face.

"You didn't, and it didn't. She sounds like she's only doing me a favour."

Ayla shrugged. "She wouldn't have agreed to see you if somewhere deep down she didn't want to see you as well." She started kissing the air. "I bet she misses you and wants to tell you she loves you, and she—"

Chase pushed a hand through her face. "Calm down there love-bot."

"I'm not a robot, I'm an AI. There's like a gazillion differences."

Chase rolled his eyes. "When we get there are you going to be able to give us some privacy? No kissy face and no jokes?"

She saluted. "Aye, aye, captain."

Chase scrunched his face. "You are the weirdest girl I've ever met."

"Girl. See? It's already like I'm human." She twirled around and her light hair became darker, and her clothes morphed into a summery dress. "This feels like me—for now."

"Glad we got all of that out of the way." Chase rolled his eyes. "Come on, or we're going to be late."

Chapter 12:
Marin Can't Be Mad, Right?

Marin wanted to meet up in one of the higher-end districts of the city, which was weird. Usually, she'd make fun of the people that lived in those sections for caring more about things than they did people. He couldn't blame her for that—that was exactly how most people there acted.

There wasn't a single reason Chase could think of, for why she'd be somewhere like that. It probably had something to do with some kind of Vanguard mission.

A visor map popped up as he approached the meeting spot. He was right on time, as always, which meant Marin would likely be another five minutes or so.

A link to a news story about an explosion at a lab in the city caught his attention. That had to be about his mission.

"Already making the news," Chase groaned. "Just, not exactly how I was hoping."

Ayla flew out of his bracelet and cocked her head. "You'll all be front-page heroes in no time! Everyone has off days."

"Yeah, yeah, yeah."

He swiped the interface away and looked up at the extravagant buildings. Every portion of the richer districts felt safe every hour of every day, but if you were in the slums, you'd be lucky to not run into a problem after and even before sun-down.

Only a couple of miles separated the sections, and the vast difference was incomprehensible to Chase.

"Well if it isn't Sellea City's resident superhero."

Marin darted out from behind a nearby building. She had what looked like a brand new burgundy leather jacket. It filled out the remainder of her look well, and it felt like she'd been missing that as a part of her image. It was clear from her scowl that she wasn't the happiest to see him.

"Everything's going to be fine. Relax." Ayla leaned closer to Chase. "Your heartbeat spiked the same way it did when you saw Zeal. If you're not careful, I'm going to start thinking you're in love with him instead of her."

Chase gave her a dull look. "Can you give us some privacy, please?"

"Jeez. All I do is try to help and this is the thanks I get?" She flew back into the bracelet.

He brought a hand to his face. "Thank you, Ayla."

Marin chuckled as she approached. "Still not used to seeing a woman jump into your wrist."

He rubbed the back of his neck. "Honestly, same"

"What is it that you wanted?" She crossed her arms. "I don't have a lot of time to chat."

Her dismissive tone told Chase she was pissed at him. She'd always been the type to hold on to anger against people she thought had wronged her. He should have brought a burger for her or something—food always helped with the apology process.

"Good to see you too. Missed you." Chase started in a sarcastic tone. "Please fill me in on all the things I've missed since we've last seen each other."

Marin rolled her eyes. "Am I supposed to want to hear what you've been up to since you ditched the Vanguard the other day?"

"Well, no," Chase shrugged. "But you can pretend to be a little excited to see me."

"Already full of yourself. Glad to see the hero life hasn't changed you."

Chase smirked, "You can't honestly say I'm any different from the usual." Marin struggled to hold back a smile. "Gotcha."

"Shut up, you jerk." She wrapped her arms around him.

As they embraced, he could feel her heart beating just as fast as his. She was holding him tighter than usual, and he hoped it was because she missed him and didn't want to admit it. They'd spent almost every day together for the last few years, so long as that didn't involve a visit to Tish, so even a day or two from each other could feel strange.

Chase flicked her new jacket as she stepped back. "Digging the jacket. Very you."

"Right?" She held the ends out and spun around. "The Vanguard got a secret new sponsor, and they decked us out with some new clothes."

Chase raised an eyebrow. "New sponsor, or new member being forced to pay for their membership?"

Marin's smile morphed into a frown. "The clothes are from a company that support the work we're doing. I can't believe you're still stuck on that." She opened her visor to check the time. "Come, walk with me."

Chase followed her down the street. "I'm kind of having a hard time."

A smirk crawled across her face. "Well, anyone leaves me—they're going to have a hard time. Ayla's gonna need time to adjust to doing everything for you."

Ain't that right.

Chase rolled his eyes. "Shut up, Ayla."

Marin stared at him in confusion before checking around for Ayla. Chase tapped his head. "We can talk just through my thoughts, but she hears everything I say too."

"She agreed with me," Marin gave him a smug look. "Didn't she?"

"You two are pretty similar."

Marin started counting on her fingers. "Pretty hot, won't put up with your crap, right most of the time. If that all sounds right, then yeah, we must be pretty similar."

She was annoying, but Chase missed being annoyed by her. "Right."

"So what's it like being a superhero? Haven't seen you flying around, so it can't be *that* great."

That was a weird thought. Chase really was a bit of superhero. His first job was a mess, but if he got into the swing of things, he knew he could do some amazing things.

Chase scratched his neck. "Honestly, the team's first mission didn't go—great. People died—there was an explosion—"

She smacked his arm. "That was you? Are you okay?"

"Not if you keep hitting me like that." Chase nodded. "I'm okay. pretty sure my kit could protect me from a nuclear bomb at this point."

Marin checked something on her visor. "How is it that you're always getting yourself into situations like that? How many people do you know that have so casually blown up or taken down a giant Conk?"

Chase grinned, "I'm one of a kind."

Marin looked down the street. "So how does your suit—kit thing work?" She pointed up to where the facility was floating in the sky. "Is it hidden up in your secret base?"

Chase slapped a hand on his bracelet. "It's just in here, like Ayla. I can use it whenever I need it."

Marin gave him a strange look. "Is that so?"

He shrugged. "I guess so—wait." Chase stopped. "How'd you know where the facility is?"

Marin cocked her head. "What do you mean? You shared your location with me when they picked you up, Chase."

He shook his head. "That would have just shown you where I was in the city. You didn't just point in it's direction. You pointed right at the facility."

Her eyes were flicking from Chase to something behind him, but he didn't care what it was.

He needed an answer, but his answer never came.

Instead, Marin pushed Chase into the middle of the road as a van came barrelling down the street.

Chapter 13:
The Freakin' Vanguard

Marin had pushed Chase hard enough to send him clean off of his feet. It felt like time slowed as he looked from Marin to the car that was headed straight for him. Chase didn't even have the time to react. His kit snapped across his body in an instant, and he knew that Ayla had done it.

The car slammed right into Chase as the kit finished covering his body—his head included, which was new to him. He could feel the metal of the car bending around his body before he shot down the street from the force of the impact.

That would have killed anyone who didn't have access to a top-secret, high-tech kit like that.

What was Marin thinking?

Ayla flew out of his kit and looked down at Chase. "Are you alright? I got everything covered in time, right?" Chase raised a thumb as he groaned and Ayla took a breath. "Thank god. What the hell just happened?"

Chase rose to his feet and stared at the van that had hit him. The front end was totaled, but the back-end was intact. Marin sauntered over to Chase as a group of people darted from nearby alleys. They all headed straight for the back of the van.

"I dunno," Chase said as he stared at the unconscious driver. "Ayla, can you scan him for his vitals?"

"Of course." She held a hand toward the van. "He's alive. He'll just have a wicked headache when he wakes up." Ayla snapped toward Marin as she approached. "What kind of friend does that to someone they love? What in the world is wrong with you?"

Ayla had stolen his words. Although, considering they were neurally linked, just what the separation between their individual words were was a bit tricky. That thought gave Chase a thousand new questions he knew he didn't have the time to ask.

Marin shrugged. "He said he could survive a nuclear blast in that thing, and I wanted to see if it was true."

Chase looked from the people at the back of the van to Marin. "Liar. This is a Vanguard mission. You just used me to stop a target."

Marin tapped her foot. "Why couldn't you have been this observant when we were working together?"

"Just cut the crap and tell me what you're doing."

"You couldn't have stopped the van any other way?" Ayla actually spat at Marin, which surprised Chase, but the saliva didn't hit the floor. "I don't like her anymore."

Marin rolled her eyes. "Oh, how the program wounds me." She beckoned Chase toward her as she headed toward the van. "Come take a look. I think you'll get a kick out of this."

Chase tried to nudge Ayla as they followed Marin. "Now look who's forgetting I'm not human."

"Cool off, okay? Marin's gotta have a good reason for that. Whoever the dude driving this thing is, he probably stole a bunch of equipment from the Vanguard or something."

Ayla cocked her head. "That a pretty common occurrence?"

"More than you'd think."

They made it around to the back of the van and watched as the crew members struggled to grab boxes. They rushed back to the vehicles they had hidden in a nearby alley and loaded them up.

There weren't any markings on any of the boxes, but there were a ton of them.

"What am I looking at?" Chase asked.

Ayla stared at the boxes and she spoke at the same time as Marin, "Medical supplies."

He looked back and forth between the two. "Medical supplies? This guy broke into the Vanguard headquarters and snuck all of this past all the medics?"

Marin looked away. "Not exactly."

"Not exactly?"

Ayla stormed toward Marin. "These aren't stolen supplies. They're supplies that are *being* stolen. Isn't that right, Marin?"

What Ayla said made sense.

Stealing supplies from the Vanguard was one thing, but medicine and food were the hardest thing to steal in the headquarters. It was hard for most people to exit the building without being searched, let alone a complete stranger walking in and taking what they wanted.

The Vanguard had been shifting into a direction Chase didn't like, but this was something else entirely. Forcing new members to pay their way into the Vanguard was scummy. Stealing supplies from a business, or a hospital, or even a family that needed them was downright pathetic.

Marin hid a guilty look with a wave of her hand. "Think of it as—the Vanguard is appropriating the necessary supplies to keep our ever-expanding roster happy and healthy."

Chase slammed the van doors shut as more crew members moved in for more supplies. "You're done. Get the hell out of here."

All the Vanguard members stared at Chase. He didn't recognize any of them, but it looked like they were sizing him up. The strange looks on some of their faces told him that they weren't quite sure what to make of his kit.

"Chase, we need these supplies," Marin said.

"Where are they headed?"

She stumbled through her words, "Well—we aren't —really entirely sure."

"And you don't see a problem with that? These could be going to any of the hospitals in the city, or to a clinic in the slums. If you guys run around doing stupid things, you need to deal with the consequences."

Marin scoffed and pointed at his hand. "Remember when you broke that?"

"Yeah, I do. I also remember refusing painkillers for it so they could go to someone who needed them more."

Chase stared at Marin. Stealing medication didn't seem like something she'd do, but she had been going on her own missions more and more the last few months. If she was so nonchalant about something like theft, it couldn't be the first time she'd done it.

"I'm going to ask what Chase doesn't want to." Ayla floated over to Marin. "How many times have you done this?"

"Obviously this isn't the first time." One of the crew members ran over and tossed Marin's crossbow to her. "Does it really matter how many times? Would a number really make anything different?"

"We joined the Vanguard to help people—not rob them." He couldn't believe what he had just heard. "All of you, get out of here now. I'm calling for help."

"You can't do that—" one of the crew members said.

Marin held her hand up to quiet them. "We need the rest of the supplies."

Chase glared at her. "You're lucky I'm even letting you go with what you have."

"It's just one dude with some chick. We can deal with him." a crew member said.

"Yeah. This guy thinks he can screw with the Vanguard? He's got another thing coming," another said.

Marin stared at her crew. "You are aware this is Chase, right? He'd beat all of you without breaking a sweat, and that's before he got some kind of super suit."

"Kit," Ayla corrected.

"Whatever."

"Even better reason to kick his ass," a crew member spat. "He's a deserter."

The crew closed in and Ayla flew into Chase's kit as he readied himself for a brawl. "I'm not going to let you take these supplies."

One of the men rushed forward and Chase met him with a foot to the chest. He managed to knock the guy off his feet, and he slammed him to the ground with his foot.

Another one rushed forward with a knife in hand, and Chase hoisted him over his head. He tossed him toward a couple of the other's and they all tumbled to the ground.

A woman rushed in with a flurry of strikes, but with the kit, it felt as if she were moving in slow-motion.

Chase blocked a strike and sent her flying with a light tap from his fist. Everyone stopped and stared at just how far the woman had flown. They were thinking twice about pushing the attack any further.

"That's enough!" Marin barked at her crew.

One man stood up and rubbed his head. "Fine. He's not even worth it. Gotta keep our strength up for that facility raid—" The rest of the crew ran back to their vehicles.

Chase watched Marin's eyes bug out. "Marin, what *facility raid* is that idiot talking about." He thought back to how she managed to point directly at the Interceptor facility. "You aren't—"

Marin avoided his gaze. "It was Tish's call."

"And you're going through with it?"

"I'm just doing what I'm told."

"You've done a lot of things I've disagreed with, but this has got to be the worst one." Chase got in her face. "Do you understand what's going to happen if you go through with that?"

"We can take care of ourselves," Marin scoffed. "You don't think we have a plan?"

"No. I bet you do. And even without me, I bet it's a stupid one. Don't do it."

Something about Marin had changed. She didn't care what the consequences of her actions might be. Tish had warped her mind into thinking that attacking a floating government facility was actually a good idea somehow.

Marin headed toward the rest of her crew. "See you soon, Chase."

He watched her go, but he wished she'd stay. It didn't feel right—he could have talked her out of it. Chase just needed some more time.

Maybe he was kidding himself.

Marin was as headstrong as people come.

Chase let the kit slide back into the bracelet as Ayla jumped out. "You okay?" Chase nodded. "What are we gonna do? Are we going to have to fight her?"

"I'm not really sure." Chase watched as Marin got in the vehicle with her crew and they drove off. "We need to get back up there and tell the team."

"What do you think they want?"

"If I had to guess, I'd probably say weapons. If Marin and Dante explained what these gauntlets can do, Tish'd be thinking about what else might be in the facility." Chase balled his fists. "I figure there's probably some more toys that are just as—explosive as these bad boys?"

Ayla nodded. "Everything up there is top of the line. You won't find anything like it anywhere else in the world."

Chase brought a hand to his chin. "That means they'll be launching a serious attack." He looked up to where the facility was nestled in the sky. "Let's get back there. It's going to suck, but I can feel an apology coming on."

Chapter 14:
Things Get Real Bad

Chase finally caught a break when he found out that Sable and Dorian were both still up at the facility. He caught even more of a break when Ayla offered to speak to Kyrie's AI, Delaynie. Odds are, if they had hopped on a call together, it would have ended in screaming and there would have been no way to get Kyrie back to the facility.

The real nuisance was waiting for Griffin to send out rides. There had to be a better way to get to and from the facility. Chase lost a lot of time just waiting to get back.

When he made it back to the facility, Griffin was waiting for him with a big smile. "I'm glad everyone's cooled off, and we can finally start—"

"We have a big problem."

Griffin's face might as well have melted. "So that's a no to everyone being cooled off?"

"The Vanguard is planning to attack the facility."

"What? When?"

"I don't know—soon. I need to talk to Sable and Dorian."

Griffin jerked his head toward the building. "I'll take you to them. What about Kyrie?"

Chase rubbed his neck as he walked alongside him. "That's probably gonna be the biggest problem, but—"

Ayla flew out of the bracelet and walked beside them. "I talked with Delaynie. They're on their way back." She twirled around and took the appearance of a friendly guidance counsellor, complete with a clipboard. "We'll fill all of you in and then we'll give him the quick version while we attempt to make sure they don't all try to kill each other again." She turned her attention to Chase. "No more fighting, right?"

The last thing Chase needed was to end up on the wrong side of any of the others' elements again. If that fight was a one time thing that would have been just fine, but something told Chase that the average sparring match would end up just as heated.

He narrowed his eyes. "It was *my* idea to come back and try to fix things."

She giggled. "Just making sure."

He turned his attention back to Griffin. "What have those two been up to since we left?"

"Well, after explaining they were going to go and eat their feelings away, they decided to take some time to ease their minds."

Chase had to stifle a laugh. Maybe a lot of the team's fight came down to a bunch of depressed, hangry people needing to cool off and eat something.

Chase scratched his head. "Ease their minds?"

"Sitting in our conservatory was their idea of relaxing."

Conservatory?

He stared at Griffin, but Ayla spoke, "Chase doesn't know what a conservatory is."

Chase's face became hot. "Ayla! C'mon! You can't go around doing that."

"It's alright," Griffin chuckled. "There isn't much greenery down in Sellea City—there hasn't been for years. I can't blame most people for not knowing." He gestured to a tree surrounded by bright flowers as they headed through a set of doors. "Our conservatory is home to some rather exotic flora. Some of the most beautiful nature you'll ever have the pleasure to experience."

Chase scoffed. "So, flowers? What a bunch of weirdos. Who'd wanna just sit in the middle of a bunch of flowers."

Ayla glared at him. "You could use some time to sit and enjoy nature. Maybe it would help you stop rushing headfirst into everything."

"I am who I am." Chase shrugged. "I'm always gonna rush into everything, keeps things fun."

Ayla sighed. "You're going to be the death of me."

"Is that how it works? I die, you die?"

"No. It's just—never mind."

Griffin led them through a few new corridors. They broke from the standard bright white corridors and instead were filled with earth tones. It was refreshing, and a hell of a lot easier on the eyes.

Chase couldn't help but wonder what kind of work the scientists got up to in the facility. Weapons and tech were one thing, but why would they need a bunch of flowers? He hadn't seen any janitors around, but maybe the flowers were to give them something else to tend to all day. There couldn't have been much cleaning required in a facility like that.

"And this," Griffin placed his hands on two frosted glass doors. "Is the conservatory."

He pushed the doors open and a wave of scents Chase had never experienced before hit him. It wasn't just smells—the array of colours were astonishing. The most wildlife down in Sellea City was the odd tree and a few plots of grass. The rainbow of flowers, plants, and even various fruits and vegetables were a treat for the eyes.

Down a well-maintained path, Chase could see Sable sitting up in a tree and Dorian with his legs crossed in a small section of flowers. They both had their eyes shut, and they each looked as if they were focused on something.

What that something could be, Chase had no clue.

He leaned toward Griffin. "What are they doing?"

"I believe they're meditating."

He sighed. "Are you guys going to make fun of me if I ask what *that* is too?"

Ayla giggled. "Maybe a little."

"You can't say anything. You're connected to pretty much everything. I'd be shocked if there was something you didn't know."

"They are simply trying to clear their minds and get in tune with their bodies." Griffin tapped his finger on a nearby panel and the various plants were doused with a fresh sprinkle of water. "It's a good technique to calm down, and the peaceful surrounding certainly help with that."

That sounded kinda groovy, but nothing Chase would be interested in. The only time he could sit around for more than five minutes was if he was admiring a view or playing one of his favourite video games.

"So, is it a bad thing if we bother them?" Chase asked.

Dorian popped an eye open. "It's a little hard to not be bothered when all of you are talking so loud!"

Ayla shrunk down and stood on Chase's shoulder. "Yikes."

Clearly, the pair of them needed to meditate—or whatever a bit more because it wasn't working when it came to *calming down*.

Chase started toward them. "Sorry—It's just—we've got a problem."

Sable hopped out of the tree as he reached them. "What kind of problem? You and Kyrie ran out of things to fight over?"

"Hey, you guys were in that fight too—" Ayla and Griffin both cleared their throats with equally irritated looks. "Right. Now is not that time." Chase ran a hand along the back of his neck. "We can all fight again later. Right now, we've got an attack to worry about."

"An attack?" Dorian stood up and brushed himself off. "What kind of attack?"

"You guys heard of the Vanguard?" They both nodded. "Well, I kinda used to run with them back in the day, and I kinda just found out that they're planning to attack the facility."

Sable gave a confused look. "This place is cloaked. How could they—"

"Chase wanted to make sure everything was safe," Griffin cut in. "He transmitted his location to a high-ranking member of the Vanguard when we brought him up here and they must have managed to figure out we're using a cluster of clouds as camouflage."

Dorian narrowed his eyes. "So, our fearless leader managed to create another problem."

Chase was ready to lay into Dorian, but Ayla spoke first. "They are a crafty bunch. Even if he hadn't done what he did—which may I remind you, was for his safety —they probably would have tracked him at some point to find the location."

"What is it they're after?"

"Weapons," Chase said as he ran a hand along his gauntlet. "Probably whatever tech they can get their hands on too, but I'd guess the primary target is weapons. Whatever makes their mission easier."

Sable raised an eyebrow. "And what's their mission?"

"Same as ours. Protect the people."

"Attacking a government facility isn't exactly protecting the people."

Chase could feel himself becoming more annoyed, but the vibrant room and exotic scents were keeping him calm. "I tried telling them that."

"How long do we have?"

"They said—" The doors behind Chase burst open and Kyrie stormed in. "Oh, good. This'll be fun."

"What's this I hear about our fearless leader screwing up, yet again?" Kyrie asked.

Dorian raised a hand. "That's basically what I said."

The sass was getting a bit much. Ayla's sass was one thing, Marin's was something else entirely, but dealing with Dorian and Kyrie was getting old fast.

Kyrie shrugged. "At least some of us are on the same page then."

Out of the corner of Chase's eye, Griffin was twitching. "Griffin, you okay?"

"ENOUGH!" Griffin snarled. "You were all selected to be a team. To come together and protect people. You weren't selected to waste time and resources while you get snippy with each other." Griffin kicked the head of a flower across the room. "None of you have any idea how serious of a threat we—the world is facing right now. Zeal is only a few big wins away from being able to wipe out humanity, and all any of you care about is your egos." He gave everyone one last look. "As far as I'm concerned, none of you deserve to even begin calling yourselves heroes."

Griffin's sudden outburst shocked the others, but it wasn't all that surprising to Chase. He'd seen small bursts of this before. Griffin was fed up—it almost felt as if he'd given up hope on his *team*.

Sable's head cocked. "Griffin—are your eyes okay?"

"What?" Ayla looked like she'd forgotten to turn her stove off. She flew over to Griffin, but he looked as if he didn't want to be seen by anyone.

He shrunk back from her and covered his eyes. "I'm fine. I just—I'm just fed up. I believed in this—In all of you. You failed just as I—" He looked toward the door. "I—I need to go now. I have—things that—that need to be done."

Chase stared at him. "What about the impending attack on the facility?"

"You're the team." Griffin stormed toward the doors. "Team up, and figure it out."

There was a feeling of defeat hanging in the air. They'd disappointed Griffin to the point of shouting. He believed in them more than anything, and they'd let him down time after time—before they even really got started.

As Griffin left, Kyrie stuck a thumb toward the doors. "What the hell was that all about?"

Sable and Dorian looked at each other. "It looked like his brain was having some kind of malfunction."

Chase raised an eyebrow. "Ayla?"

"I'm not sure." She shook her head. "I've never seen anything like that before."

"You saw his eyes, though, right?" Sable asked. "They looked like they were like, yellow for a second there."

Chase brought a hand to his chin. "Maybe someone should keep an eye on him."

Ayla put her hands on her hips. "Are you all going to be able to not kill each other while I'm gone?"

Kyrie glared at Chase. "If this threat is as serious as you said, I can wait to kick his ass some more."

Ayla smiled. "Good. You bunch of psychos can talk things over while I go spy on Griff." She flashed a peace sign at Chase. "Be right back." She disappeared in a small flash.

"So what's the situation?" Kyrie asked.

"Everyone's still got all their gear with them, right? Kit's at the ready?" Chase asked, and everyone responded with a nod. "Good, because the Vanguard is planning to attack and we need to be ready for a fight."

Kyrie gave everyone a confused look. "What the hell do they think the point of that is?"

"You missed the big pow-wow. The point is, we're looking at an army of do-gooders set to make their way up here at any point."

Delaynie appeared beside Kyrie. "Sooner than you may think. Multiple vehicles just broke from the sky lanes and are headed directly toward us."

"Crap."

Dorian flicked out his scythe and twirled it. "So what's the plan?"

Kyrie stepped forward. "I think we——" Chase cleared his throat. "Whatever. Take the floor, leader."

"Since they're probably coming for gear, we need to make sure they can't make it into the facility, and we probably need to protect any of the scientists from abduction."

Sable narrowed her eyes. "I thought the Vanguard didn't do stuff like that."

"I thought so too."

Chase couldn't hide the disappointment in his voice. At least the rest of the team wouldn't know the exact source of his disappointment. It might be a little embarrassing if they knew he was more upset about Marin's actions than he was about the actions of the Vanguard.

Kyrie cracked his neck. "How's about I send Delaynie to run any defence systems we have available, then you two can send your AI to rally anyone up here capable of fighting to come and help us." Delaynie nodded and disappeared before Kyrie even finished. "The Vanguard may be stupid, but they aren't going to actually try to kill anyone, right?"

Chase crossed his arms. "That's a good idea," Dorian and Sable each nodded and sent their AI's off into the facility. "But I'm not actually sure whether or not they're going to go easy on us. They've changed a lot in a short amount of time."

Ayla appeared beside Chase with a feed of Griffin alongside her. He was typing at some kind of console. "We've got another problem."

That was just what the team needed. More issues in the midst of what was already a pretty major issue.

Chase groaned, "What now? We don't need to know about Griff's visor history—" Ayla raised an eyebrow at him. "Sorry—what's going on?"

"Well, Griffin is currently in the middle of transferring that program data you all recovered from the Yorks."

Dorian looked furious. "What? He's betraying us? That piece of—"

Sable held a hand up. "We don't know he's betraying us. He was acting weird. Something must be wrong. Maybe he's worried the Vanguard will get their hands on it."

Ayla shook her head. "I can't trace where the transfer is going. Some kind of encryption, and there's only one person I know that has tech comparable to us."

"Zeal." Chase balled his fists. "Can you stop the transfer?"

"Not without shutting the entire system down."

"Do it."

"That'll just bring Zeal right to our front door, especially if he sees that we're already getting attacked.

He'll use the confusion to get in and get the rest of the data."

Dorian laughed. "Not like we have any other options right now."

Chase shrugged. "He's right. If we cut the computer systems, will we still have access to any defence systems in the facility?"

"Defence systems run separately from our main computers," Ayla said as she brought a finger to her lip. "Just in case we were to get EMP'd and need some kind of back-up. Highly complex stuff, but if we do that then the cloaking on the facility will be gone. We'll be on display for the whole world to see and—"

Chase held a hand up. "So that's a yes?"

"Yes."

"Cut the systems."

Ayla looked as if she had zoned out, but the console Griffin was typing at shut off. For whatever reason, Griffin had stopped moving as well.

Chase tilted his head. "Is he okay?"

"You asked me to wipe out all the computer systems for now. I did."

Sable gasped, "So you're saying—"

Dorian laughed and shook his head. "The weirdo's been a bot the entire time?"

The thought hadn't even crossed Chase's mind.

It made sense the more he thought about it. How much hitting Griffin hurt that first day when they fought. His strange outburst, the way he spoke, the weird thing with his eyes.

All the clues were there.

Chase had just been too wrapped up in his own world to notice them.

"But, how would Zeal have gotten Griffin on his side?" Sable asked. "When has he ever been around him?"

Ayla spun around and her form shifted into a menacing shadow creature. "You can do some crazy stuff remotely." She spun again and returned to her usual look. "I'm unable to access his systems, but if I had to guess, Zeal got to him early—like, when he was being made early."

Kyrie scoffed, "Any other android, robot—whatever's running around that you wanna tell us about?"

Ayla smiled like she wasn't aware of the gravity of the situation. "Nope, just Griff."

"Great. We gotta get out there." Chase headed for the door and the others followed.

Kyrie moved beside him. "I'm pretty confident in our ability to beat up the Vanguard, but what are we going to do when Zeal arrives? The four of us can't fight two armies *and* protect that console."

"He's right," Sable said. "It's either the program data or the weapons and tech."

Sable and Kyrie were right. The team was in a tight place. Both options could lead to horrific outcomes. Even worse, both outcomes would end up being wins for Zeal.

There had to be a way to stop everyone. Some way to sabotage things.

Chase smirked. "Ayla, how are you with building viruses?"

Ayla's look told Chase she knew what he was getting at. "I'm on it."

BOOM!

The entirety of the facility shook. From the sounds of that explosion, the Vanguard was coming with everything they had. To his surprise, Chase wasn't worried about potentially beating up people he used to call friends. Tish probably would have been fun to smack around after all the fights and disagreements they'd had throughout the years.

He was only worried about Marin.

But there wasn't any time to think about that.

The Vanguard had arrived.

They were out of time.

Chapter 15:
Falling For Marin

As the team made it back out to the front of the facility, the Vanguard piled out of their vehicles. It looked like there were almost one hundred different Vanguard members, which put Chase at ease. He figured they would have rallied the entirety of the Vanguard for an attack, but maybe they had underestimated the scope of the facility.

Tish stepped forward from the group. "Chase, tell your team to stand down, and there won't be any problems."

Chase rolled his eyes, but Kyrie spoke first, "We aren't taking orders from some random Vanguard woman."

"Random Vanguard woman? I'm hurt. You mean, Chase never mentioned even a single thing about me?"

Everyone looked at Chase and he shrugged. "She's the leader of the Vanguard—also a giant pain in the ass."

"And do you know her—" Sable raised an eyebrow. "Or do you *know* her?"

The thought of being with Tish like that launched his body into an involuntary shudder. She wasn't an atrocious-looking woman, but she was far from anyone Chase would ever be interested in. Her brand of bossy was a bit too out there when compared to someone like Marin.

"She was basically my boss. That's it." Chase turned back to Tish. "And honestly, not a very good one."

"You're just sour we figured out where your facility is."

"Pretty sure I'm sour that you guys were literally stealing medical supplies the other night." His eyes fell on Marin. "Obviously, it wasn't the first time either."

Tish shrugged. "We do what we have to do in order to protect the people of the city. Why else do you think we'd be coming here?"

Dorian readied his scythe. "To steal out tech."

Tish looked confused. "Well, yes. That's kind of what I was getting at."

Sable drew her sword. "That's not what real heroes do."

"Are you kidding me with these people, Chase? They're like bloody fairytale characters." Tish brought a hand to her face. "We're here to procure your weapons and tech so we can better defend the city from Zeal. I hear that explosion the other night might as well be your fault."

Kyrie pulled his staff and leaned toward the rest of the team. "So, what? Twenty-something people each? Sounds manageable." He flicked the end of his staff toward Tish. "Dibs on the ring leader."

For one of the first times since Chase had known him, Kyrie said something he liked. Despite how much they butted heads, the two of them did have one thing in common, they loved a chaotic fight.

Chase raised an eyebrow as his kit covered his body. "Is that confidence or overconfidence?"

"Don't worry," Kyrie nodded toward Marin. "I'll help you with yours when I'm done with mine."

"Overconfidence it is."

"Forget it." Tish looked at her men. "Take them down."

A pause fell over the soon-to-be battlefield. The Vanguard weren't entirely sure what they were in for. Some people were practically snarling, but others looked like they were afraid.

Chase looked at his own team, but there wasn't a hint of fear on any of them.

Marin rushed from the crowd and Chase ran right toward her. Luckily, whatever security force the facility had on hand had managed to come to help with the struggle. It wasn't going to be an easy fight, but knowing that they had some extra help with protecting the facility entrance put Chase's mind at ease.

As he reached Marin, he was surprised to find that she hadn't brought her new crossbow. Instead, she'd brought a strange baseball bat. Even if it didn't look so strange, Chase would have assumed that it was custom-made. It only resembled a bat in terms of shape, not in design.

She took a swing toward him, but mid-swing something inside the bat seemed to ignite and it exploded with even more force.

He dodged it, but the force of the swing pushed him back from the blast of air it created. He'd never seen a weapon like that before.

"Another new weapon." Chase raised his fists. "Steal that one from some up-and-coming inventor?"

She looked at the bat. "Something like that."

We've got another problem.

Tell me something new.

Okay—I think Marin has her own AI.

What? How would she—

Marin lashed out with a few quick strikes that Chase flipped away from, but the other Vanguard members took that as their opportunity to strike. Grunts on each side of Chase grabbed his wrists and pulled tight. Marin started toward him as she twirled her bat again.

Ayla?

Shields. Get ready.

Each of the grunt's hands shot away from Chase as the two circular shields formed on his wrists. He spun and nailed one with a wicked kick as he smashed a shield into the face of the other.

Marin raised her bat, but Chase replied by launching a grappling hook at it. Ayla disconnected it from his kit and Marin deflected it. The slight distraction was enough for Chase to close in and he hit Marin with a body blow that sent her flying backward.

Kyrie and Tish's fight caught his attention.

Both of them were using a staff, but at first, it wasn't clear who was more skilled. Tish had to be the better fighter because she was keeping the pressure on Kyrie despite her lack of a kit or an element.

It was rare enough to see her in combat while Chase was with the Vanguard, so seeing her fight was actually a serious treat.

He turned his attention back to Marin. She ran a hand through her hair and tapped her bat along the ground. The hit had taken a toll on her body, but she kept her confident smirk.

They locked eyes again, but Chase needed answers. "Ayla says you have an AI—that true?"

Marin looked like the question had caught her off guard, but she flipped right back into her usual cool, confidence. "It certainly is." She held out a hand with her palm to the sky, and a small red AI appeared. "Meet, Alyx. I'm not quite sure how AI relations work, but you could say that he's—"

"Ayla's brother."

My what?

"I can see why you like Ayla. Having an all-knowing piece of tech with you at all times really is a big help. He was even able to help confirm our suspicions about the exact location of this little facility."

Chase thought back to the night he and Marin had taken the tech to Dante. He said he was just scanning his gauntlets and the AI disk, but he was copying the files. He must have copied the program data running through the gauntlets tech as he downloaded Alyx's AI off the disk. That means that the bat—

"So your fancy little bat is just a crappier version of my gauntlets, huh?"

Marin smiled. "We couldn't quite work out all the kinks for our own pair of gauntlets without someone blowing themselves up, so we settled on this." She twirled the bat. "Like it?"

"I'm going to like taking it from you."

"Come and try."

Ayla activated his thrusters, and he clobbered a couple of random Vanguard grunts as he made his way over to Marin.

He caught a glimpse of the others and it looked like they were all having the time of their lives. Sable and Dorian were back to back sending people flying in every direction, while Kyrie battled against Tish. Even the security group that had arrived to help the team seemed like they were having fun.

Chase threw a heavy shot at Marin, but she ducked it and whacked her bat across his knee.

He dropped from the shock of the pain.

If that bat hit anyone without a kit, they were a goner.

She swung the bat at him, but he met it with one of his wrist shields, shattering the shield the instant they met.

She kept swinging over and over, pushing Chase backward. Marin was trying to push Chase toward the edge of the facility.

They both knew that as terrifying as the drop was, Chase would be able to survive it. The wide swings made it hard to dodge around her. If one of the swings caught him, he'd end up getting shot off the facility.

He needed to think of something.

This—Alyx thing is the only reason she's striking with such precision.

You able to do something about it?

His data structure is flawed. I think I can scramble his data for just a second, but you need to be ready.

Chase smirked.

Go for it.

After a wide swing from Marin, her eyes bugged out and she faltered. Chase took the opportunity to dive behind her and give her a little boot toward the edge. He feared he had kicked her a bit too hard, but she recovered.

She swung the bat around as she got back to her feet. "Nice move. Bit cheap, but still nice." She looked behind her at the huge drop to the city below. "You gonna throw me off?"

Chase shook his head. "You're going to put the bat down, and tell everyone to stand down."

"For what? So you can arrest me and the rest of the Vanguard? Who do you think that's going to help?"

"I'm serious, Marin." Chase balled his fists. "Final warning."

She scoffed, "We both know I can take—" A sudden bolt of electricity flew in and struck Marin, sending her sprawling off the floating facility.

She was gone...

Chapter 16:
That's A Promise

One second, she was there. The next second, all Chase had was his memories of her.

He couldn't hear himself say it, but he knew he had spoken. "Ma—Marin?"

There was a moment where they locked eyes.

Right before she disappeared.

Marin's face was covered in a fearful look.

Was that how she'd spend the last moments of her life?

Speeding toward the city below, terrified?

That's not the way she deserved to die.

She deserved a long, happy life. A life anyone would be jealous of. A life where she got to go out on her terms, surrounded by family.

He was going into a state of shock.

His heart was racing, and it was like everything around him had disappeared. The sounds of a battlefield were replaced by Marin's voice echoing around in Chase's head.

He moved toward the edge without thinking, but the tight grip of a hand held him back. He wasn't sure who it was, he didn't care. Part of him wanted to dive over the edge and do everything he could to save Marin, but was it even possible at that point? Had too much time passed?

Marin's screams didn't even last all that long. They trailed off far faster than he would have thought possible.

He turned and saw that Kyrie had stopped him. He was yelling something at him, but Chase couldn't make out the words. Kyrie's eyes focused on something else and he dodged out of the way of a staff strike from Tish.

She looked at Chase's for a moment, and it almost looked like she felt a sense of pity and despair. Whatever the reason, she didn't take the opportunity to toss him off the facility as well.

Chase thought back to the first time he and Marin responded to a group of Conks in the city. They were targeting a bunch of random rich business tycoons on one of their rooftop paradises. After a long fight, they figured they'd finally bashed up the last of the Conks, but they had missed one. It knocked Chase right over the edge of the building.

There couldn't have been much time to react to something like that—

But Marin did.

She practically threw herself off the building to catch him. She wrapped her hand tight around his wrist as she held onto the railing for dear life.

She didn't think about it—she just did it.

Chase hadn't returned the favour.

He failed her.

Sickening laughter brought Chase back to reality, "AHAHAHAHAHA!"

Chase pulled his eyes from the edge of the facility and he scanned toward where the bolt of electricity had come from. The familiar figure of Zeal hovered above a small army of his Conks.

He was staring right back at Chase with an insane grin.

Zeal had knocked Marin off the facility.

Zeal had killed his best friend.

The woman that he—

"If nothing else comes from today, that's one less nuisance in this world." Zeal looked down his nose at Chase. "Good riddance."

The rest of his senses started to return as he stared up at Zeal with eyes filled with hatred.

Chase? Hey, come on—talk to me.

"I'm gonna kill him."

Chapter 17:
A Bad Day For The Vanguard

Chase shot toward Zeal but was met with a wave of Conks that blocked his path. He launched his fist into the unfortunate bot that stopped in front of him and it shot back like a rocket. The others managed to deflect the bot into the air and off of the facility.

Even Zeal's own forces didn't care about their numbers.

They were nothing but replaceable hunks of scrap.

Zeal pulled a small device from his coat and pushed a button. A wave of energy passed over the entirety of the facility. Chase knew what he'd just done—it was exactly what Ayla had said. Zeal came here to restore functionality to the computers so he could get his hands on the program data.

The data the Yorks died to protect.

Chase stopped when he heard Tish, "Everyone! Focus on the Conks! That bastard killed Marin."

He looked around at the Vanguard as they turned their attention to Zeal. They looked even more afraid than they had when they were preparing to attack the team.

One man took a shaky step forward. "For Marin."

"FOR MARIN!" The entire crowd replied before the Vanguard clashed with the sea of Conks.

It was touching to see how much Marin meant to the Vanguard. All of those people were willing to die in her name.

A Conk's arm morphed into a sword and it swung at Chase. He ducked it and threw a heavy kick, aided by the thrusters of his kit. The Conk flew up into the air, but Sable met it and sliced it clean in half.

As Chase prepared to take Zeal down, a group of giant Conk's, like the one he'd fought back before all the Interceptor craziness started, teleported in front of him. "If anyone's available, I'm probably gonna need some help here."

From behind the giant Conks, he saw Tish sprinting toward Zeal. She knocked down a group of Conks and then vaulted herself up to him. They both fell back to the ground and rolled, but Tish was back up in an instant.

Kyrie nudged Chase as he took a stance beside him. "We've got this."

Chase nodded. "We do."

One of the Conks launched a huge fist toward them, but Kyrie planted his staff into the ground with force. It was angled in such a way that as the fist connected, it sent the Conk's arm up. Chase took the opening and launched toward it, sending a huge punch of his own into the Conk. The bot's head flew right off its shoulders and knocked down a few of the smaller Conks.

Chase was in the air with nowhere to go as another fist barrelled toward him. He tensed his body to prepare for the impact, but he saw Kyrie launch toward him.

He held the end of his staff out and Chase grabbed onto it. Kyrie used the momentum to toss Chase right at the Conk and as his fist met the Conk's, the arm flew off of its body.

They both landed on the ground and Kyrie flashed a thumb. "Buncha chumps."

Two giant Conk's lumbered toward them, and they each prepared for another round. Two quick slashes cut through each of the Conk's heads and Sable and Dorian landed beside them.

Sable wiped a bit of fluid from her blade. "Heard you boys needed some help."

Kyrie smiled as he jutted a thumb toward Chase. "That was him. Not me."

Chase could tell it wasn't meant to be a dickish comment. It felt more like playful banter. Banter between a pair of friends.

"Everyone good? I have a feeling we're gonna need to work together to beat—"

"AAARGGH!"

Tish's anguished screams caught everyone's attention.

What had happened to her wasn't clear at a glance, but as the blood started to pour from her body, things became clear.

Zeal had run her through with a blade of his own. As he pulled it out and kicked her to the ground, something about the sword felt familiar—like he'd seen it somewhere before.

Even from the distance, Chase could see the venom in Zeal's eyes as he stalked toward Tish once more. He held a hand out and a multitude of light streaks flew from it.

Chase had no clue what was happening until he thought back to the team's run-in with Zeal. All those different colours, and the screams they were generating from Tish—the beams of light had to be concentrated forms of elements.

Zeal wasn't just using one element, though. Judging by the colours coming from his hand, he was using all of them. He reeled back and hit her hard with a kick that sent her into the air.

Sable hopped up and brought her to the ground safely. "Hey, you okay?"

Tish spat out some blood, but it didn't look like it was voluntary.

Chase took her hand. "Tish—c'mon, Tish."

She coughed and sputtered as she gripped Chase's arm. "Stop that—" He could feel her grip fade as her sputtering came to a stop.

Tish was gone.

In just a few minutes, the Vanguard was brought to its knees. Without any potential leadership, the future of the mercenaries was unclear.

Chase closed her eyes. "I will."

"She's gone, man." Kyrie put a hand on his shoulder. "Sable and Dorian are gonna need our help."

The twins had already launched themselves at Zeal. The both of them launched flurries of attacks, but Zeal wasn't having any problem keeping his distance. Every time Sable attempted to summon flames, Zeal put a quick stop to it with a wave of ice.

It was hard to tell when Dorian was using his element, but he figured Zeal had some way to avoid getting caught up in Dorian's time element.

As they rushed to help their teammates, Zeal let out a huge flash. It was like the one Griffin had used to stop the fight in the facility. It blinded Chase, so he figured it had blinded everyone else, but a sharp tug told him otherwise.

When his sight returned Sable had each of the Interceptors behind her as she held her sword toward Zeal.

The flash wasn't enough for Zeal to take the team out, but it was enough for the Conk's to surround anyone still left standing.

They were surrounded with nowhere to go.

Everyone gritted their teeth as they looked at the

army in front of them.

The odds were stacked against them.

Those were usually the kind of odds Chase liked, but this looked to be a bit too much.

Chase—

"A little busy right now."

Ayla appeared beside him. "The upload's done."

Chase smirked. "Perfect."

"KILL THEM ALL! NOW!" Zeal reared back. "AHAHAHAHA!"

Everyone prepared for a final stand—but nothing happened. All the Conks just stared at them. Their heads started to twitch and spark.

Zeal had gotten his hands on the program data, but Chase and Ayla's plan had worked. One by one the Conks started detonating until the ground was littered with Conk parts.

Zeal stared at the destruction around him, shocked by what had happened.

The Interceptors all stared up at Zeal as they raised their weapons.

It was time to finish things, once and for all.

Chapter 18:
Let's Beat Up An Old Man

"What have you done to my brilliant creations?" Zeal spat.

"Brilliant?" Dorian laughed. "Sorry to tell ya, psycho, but your little bot's are light-years away from brilliant."

Ayla grew to the size of a small building and stuck her tongue out at Zeal. "Next time you steal data, make sure it's not filled to the brim with viruses." She returned to normal size and spun until her clothes morphed to a matching kit. "Especially when those viruses are programmed to spread to any and all tech the downloader has access to."

A look of worry crossed Sable's face. "Griffin—"

Chase gave her a confident look. "Later." He turned his attention to Zeal. "Guys, how's about we do the world a kindness and beat up this old man?"

Chase ran toward Zeal, but for the first time, Kyrie put his one-upmanship to good use.

Kyrie vaulted from behind Chase, using his leaders approach as cover to close the gap on Zeal. The old man never saw it coming as Kyrie brought the staff down across his cheek.

Chase and the twins rushed into the fight as Zeal responded by blasting Kyrie with a huge bolt of electricity. the trio began launching every attack they could think of, but Zeal managed to keep up with all of them at the same time.

Sable would slash at his legs as Dorian took a shot at his back, but Zeal created ice in place of both attacks. Their weapons bounced off as the ice shattered.

Chase took a few swings, but Zeal was far more agile than he appeared. He ducked a right cross and a wave of pitch black tendrils launched out of his chest, sending Chase flying back to where Kyrie had landed.

"He must do pilates or somethin'," Chase groaned.

"Okay, we are getting our asses beat by an old man." Kyrie rose to his feet and dusted himself off. "Any ideas other than—attack?"

"Not sure. Ayla, you have any idea how we can deal with him?"

Ayla appeared beside him. "I have an idea, but you really aren't going to like it."

Zeal sent Dorian flying backward with a huge ice fist. He hit the ground hard and rolled to Chase's feet.

Dorian's eyes were wide, but he looked confused. "I think that asshole just punched me with a giant block of ice."

Chase gawked at the giant ice fist that now stood in the middle of the battlefield. "That he did."

"This is perfect!" Ayla whirled around. "Dorian is just who we need! Stay on the ground and act like you're hurt."

"What?" they all asked at the same time.

"Just listen!"

"Anytime you guys want to get back into the fight— that would be great!" Sable called as she dodged a series of ice spikes from Zeal.

"Ayla. Plan. Fast. Go," Chase said as he watched the battle.

Zeal wasn't paying all that much attention to Sable.

He was fighting her without even looking at her, but she was giving it everything she had just to stay alive.

"I think the problem is your kits. Somehow, Zeal can detect the movements of your kits as you come in for an attack." Ayla spun around until she was much smaller and riding her very own tech-cycle. "There's a weird field I can sense radiating from him detecting your Interceptor gear, but he won't detect something like this."

Kyrie gave her a confused look. "That's great, but where are we supposed to get one of those?"

Ayla looked at Chase, and the others followed suit.

"You want me to ride my tech-cycle at Zeal? Even if I got rid of my kit, wouldn't he still detect my gauntlets?"

Ayla stepped off her tech-cycle and lifted it over her head. "That's not exactly what I had in mind."

"Absolutely not." Chase shook his head. "Not my baby. Do you know how many credits I put into her?"

He'd had that thing for his entire adult life. While friends would come and go, his tech-cycle was the one constant in his life. It's hard for it to drive away on its own when it's stuck in a disk.

"We don't have any more time." Ayla said.

Zeal froze Sable's feet to the ground and began to approach her. If they didn't do something fast, Sable was a goner.

"Fine." Chase pulled out the disk housing his tech-cycle and tossed it to Dorian. "If you miss the throw you're buying me a new one."

"Then you two better get in there." Dorian beamed as he snatched the disk. "I'll wait for my opening."

"Enjoy your break, then." Kyrie rushed forward. "Punch me." He hopped in the air and placed his feet on his staff.

Chase was caught off guard but managed to strike the staff with a hard straight left, sending Kyrie rocketing toward Zeal.

Kyrie was blocked by Zeal once again, but it was enough of a distraction for Sable to get out of her tight spot.

As Chase rushed back into the fight, he wished he could have just launched his tech-cycle at Zeal the same way he had for Kyrie, but he had a feeling his ride couldn't take the initial impact. Tech-cycles were notoriously fragile.

"Nice of the strapping men to finally show up," Sable scoffed as Chase started doing everything he could to strike Zeal. "What were you doing?"

"Well—" Chase dodged a wave of dark tendrils and gave them a solid shot, sending them flying into the sky. "—I got hit by those freaky things, Kyrie got exploded with lightning, and Dorian got—fisted. There's a lot to process with everything that's going on."

"I've grown tired of this foolishness." Zeal said as he created a bit of distance.

"So you'd be willing to just head over there and hop off the facility?" Chase asked.

"It's time for you all to die."

"We'd really rather not."

Zeal exploded a combination of flames, electricity, and sharp gusts of wind, sending everyone back. It looked like Kyrie and Sable both took nasty blasts from the electricity, which worried Chase when they hit the ground without another movement.

"And I'd rather you did."

Chase turned his attention back to Zeal and prepared himself for the worst.

Zeal was headed straight for Chase with his sword in hand. He was moving so fast, there wasn't going to be anytime to dodge, and Chase's kit didn't have enough power to block it.

It would have been a miracle if Dorian somehow managed to hit Zeal with a throw, even with help from an AI.

He shut his eyes, and prepared for the end—but the end never came.

He opened his eyes as the sound of metal scraping against metal stopped in front of him. He looked up at Griffin, who looked down at him with a smile. His eyes were still a strange colour, and his entire body was in a state of spasm, but he looked happy.

"Griffin—you—"

His head jerked. "I-i-i-it was a p-p-pleasure to be able to bring you to-to-to-together."

Zeal pulled the sword out and readied another strike, but Griffin spun around and threw his body over Zeal.

Chase knew what was about to happen.

Griffin was going to try to take Zeal with him.

"LET GO OF ME YOU USELESS HUNK OF TIN!" Zeal screamed.

Griffin's body started to spark as Chase scrambled away from the two of them. "F-f-f-f-f-fuuu—"

Griffin exploded into a cloud of dust.

Chase had no idea if he had managed to take Zeal with him, but regardless, Chase appreciated the sacrifice. Somehow Griffin was able to not only fight Zeal's control but also the virus ravaging his systems in order to help Chase one last time.

If anyone was a hero on that day, it was Griffin.

Chase got back to his feet as the dust cleared, and Zeal's frustrated face peeled through the haze. The explosion didn't look like it had done much aside from irritating him. How an old man could withstand an explosion at point-blank range was anyones guess.

"How?" Chase asked through gritted teeth. "You're a monster."

"AHAHAHAHAHA!" Zeal cackled. "A monster? No —I'm much worse. I will be the end of humanity." Flames sprouted up all around him. "Starting with you."

The horrendous and beautiful sight of Chase's tech-cycle crashing into Zeal gave Chase new hope.

There was a chance.

Dorian rushed past Chase and swung his scythe at Zeal. Zeal managed to separate from the tech-cycle in the air, but he was still in a bad spot. Dorian missed him, and destroyed the tech-cycle, much to Chase's horror.

Losing his tech-cycle sucked, but it was far from the worst loss of the day.

Chase stumbled to his feet and charged toward Zeal as the old man hit the floor.

Sable slashed down at Zeal and he was in a scramble doing everything he could to avoid the strikes. A quick flash blinded her as he crawled away.

Kyrie stomped on one of Zeal's hands and pointed his staff down at him. "You're done."

"No!" Zeal tried to get up to run in the opposite direction, but Chase met him with a huge right hand, sending Zeal face-first into the ground.

Chase blew on his fist. "Yes."

Zeal rolled over and stared up at the team that surrounded him.

Sable and Dorian held the ends of their weapons toward Zeal. "Alright, eyebrows. It's over."

On the ground beneath them, he looked like nothing more than a sad old man. If someone didn't know any better, they probably wouldn't have thought anything of someone like Zeal.

"They'll turn on you," Zeal growled. "The government—the people—your own team. You'll see. YOU'LL ALL SEE! And on that day, you *will* seek me out." He looked right at Dorian and Sable. "I guarantee it." He glared at Chase. "You think you're all heroes—you know nothing. My mission is so much bigger than any single one of you could comprehend."

Then in a sudden flash of light, Zeal disappeared.

Chapter 19:
Before He Was A General

Zeal may have managed to get away with the data, but with how virus-riddled it was, it was possible that he'd never get a chance to use it.

That was the saving grace of the entire day.

He wouldn't get that program fully operational for a long, long time.

Chase looked around at the destruction.

The three factions going at it had really done a number on the facility, but the Interceptors won the day. It didn't necessarily look like it, but that didn't matter. Chase could feel a sense of pride radiating from his teammates.

Dorian put an arm around Chase. "Good call on sabotaging the program. There was no way we were going to be able to deal with all of that without something going wrong somewhere."

"I'm glad we're all alright." Chase looked toward wear Marin had fallen. "We lost enough people today."

"Of course we are!" Dorian flexed his arm. "You think a puny bot or an old man are gonna to take out the almighty Dorian?" He looked over to his sister and laughed. "I guess Sable did a good job too."

She hadn't stopped moving since the battle ended. There were plenty of wounded people scattered around, and Sable was doing what she could to assist each and every one of them. It was nice to see how much she cared for others.

"We wouldn't have had the time to come up with a plan if she wasn't able to take on Zeal by herself."

"Next time, they'll know to send two armies on top of the first one." He gave Chase a bit of a shake. "I never got to thank you, for looking out for my sister back during our first mission."

Chase raised an eyebrow. "Me? Look after her?" He scoffed. "Pretty sure she was taking care of me."

"She's a tough one, but she's the only family I've got." He let him go and held out a hand. "I'm glad I can count on you, leader."

Chase shook his hand. "She's not the only family you've got. Not sure about Kyrie, but you've got me."

"Beating up bots and I get a new brother?" He let out a huge laugh and wrapped Chase in a monstrous hug. "Best day ever."

Maybe that meditating was working out for Dorian. It felt like forever ago that they were all at each other's throats, but the truth was, it had only been a few minutes.

Chase looked over to where Griffin had sacrificed himself. "I don't really know what happens to the group now that Griffin's gone."

"It'll be fine." He gave Chase a little punch on the shoulder. "Something tells me the suits are gonna realize that things would have been a lot worse without us around."

Kyrie made his way over. "Mind if I talk to Chase real quick?"

Dorian raised an eyebrow. "You're not planning on having that one-on-one for leadership right now are you?"

"I'm over it." He shook his head. "Besides, I'm sure

I'll end up in charge eventually."

Dorian gave them each a tap. "Play nice, or me and Sable are gonna plant you both in the ground."

Kyrie didn't seem angry—he actually seemed happy. It was one of the only times Chase had seen him without a scowl on his face. It was good to see that the whole team saw that day as a victory, and not as some kind of loss.

"You good? You took some heavy hits back there," Chase said.

Kyrie rubbed his arm. "Nothing a little T-L-C won't fix." He held a hand out to Chase. "I get it now—why you're the leader. You may not always make the right call, but in the most screwed-up situations you make the best call possible—even if it means sacrificing your precious bike—"

"Tech-cycle."

"Is that what that was?" Kyrie smirked. "I may have been the first to put on a kit, but what they've all been saying is true. You're the first true Interceptor."

He shook his hand. "Thanks, Kyrie."

"I wanted to start over. You know—quit being a dick and try to get along. I never even told you guys, I don't really like being called Kyrie."

He raised an eyebrow. "What do you want us to call you?"

"I prefer to go by my last name, Odon."

"Odon." He smiled at him. "You look like an Odon."

"Hey, guys," Sable said as she and Dorian made their way over. "I've just been informed that we'll have a few days off to recuperate. Wanna go grab some post-victory grub? Government's buyin'."

Everyone nodded, but Chase thought of something. "Do you guys mind if I meet up with you? I've got something I need to do first."

Chase looked down toward Sellea City with his mind on the future. With Tish and Marin gone, the Vanguard was nothing but an aimless group of mercenaries. Luckily, the Interceptors were going to be more than enough to pick up the slack.

Chapter 20:
A Watchful Eye

Chase looked down to the rundown streets of the slums. "You said they'd be here by now."

Ayla ran a hand through her hair. "I'm an AI, not a master of human nature. They'll be here anytime."

A part of Chase was excited to see the York kids again, even if they wouldn't see him. Their recoveries had gone well, which was a relief to Chase. The thought of the kids up and running about again was a nice one.

He wished he could talk to each of them, and let them know that they would be okay without their parents —if someone had done that for him when he was young, he might not have been so bitter and closed off for much of his youth.

He wiped his sweaty palms and felt the bulge of Ayla's disk in his pocket. He pulled it out and stared at it. "Could you run a scan on the data in this?"

"Why? It'll just have some storage data and enough room for me to rest inside—"

"Ayla—"

"I'm doing it." She held a hand up to it. "It's exactly what I said. That's all there is."

That scan Dante had done back at the Vanguard headquarters had removed Alyx's data. Marin really did have her own AI. There was just no telling what an incomplete AI meant—if Marin was even still alive.

He ran his fingers across the buttons. "You said nothing would happen if this were destroyed, but what would happen to you if you were stored in here and it was destroyed?"

"If I was inside it and it were destroyed—that would be the only way to really get rid of me. That's the only time my data is unable to jump to another device or network."

"But if you aren't inside it and it were destroyed—you wouldn't be able to be destroyed, right?"

Ayla brought her hand to her chin. "You're up to something aren't you? Do I need to waste my super-duper AI power on thinking about what you're planning?"

"Thinking?"

"Do we have to do this every time?"

"It was a joke."

She narrowed her eyes. "You're already getting good at hiding your thoughts from me."

"Or am I just not thinking about anything at all?"

"Probably that one. Without any of my data in it, there'd be no way to house me without lowering my functionality. So, yeah, if it were destroyed now I'd be virtually indestructible."

Chase dropped the disk to the floor and crushed it with his foot. It was almost funny how easy it was.

Ayla stared at it with wide eyes. "What did you—"

"Now no one can ever hurt or threaten you. You'll be free to annoy the world long after I'm gone."

"I'm just an AI, Chase."

He shook his head. "No. You're Ayla. My partner. Partners protect each other. No one should ever be able to just store you away like an old video." She looked like she was ready to cry as her image started to shimmer. "Ayla, are you okay? Did something—"

She looked up at Chase and brought a hand to his

face. For just a slight moment, he could have sworn he actually felt her hand on his face. "You're stuck with me for life now. You know that right?"

Chase turned his attention back down to the street as a car arrived. "There's worse ways to live a life."

He watched as Rhys and Lenna got out of the car and stared at the rundown home they'd be spending the rest of their young lives in. They didn't look excited, and he couldn't blame them.

He smiled when he watched Rhys turn to his sister. Things looked hopeless for the kids, but rather than wallow in sadness, Rhys made his sister laugh. They were going to have it hard, but at least they had each other.

Ayla had a puzzled look on her face. "I'm really not sure why, but that kid—the boy—he's giving me the weirdest sense of deja-vu."

"Okay, you can yell at me for asking whether or not an AI can actually get deja-vu."

Ayla laughed, "No. I can't." She cocked her head. "It's strange." She looked at Chase. "Do you think they'll be alright?"

"I do." Chase smiled down at them. "Griffin put everything in place, and despite everything that happened, I trust what he did. Plus, we'll be keeping an eye on them every once in a while. Nothing wrong with them lucking out and finding some extra funds lying around if they ever need them." Chase winked.

They watched the kids disappear into the house. "Ayla, I have kind of a big thing I need to ask of you."

"Uh-oh. That doesn't sound good."

"Can you erase your—memories, I guess—of the Yorks?"

"I can on two conditions." Ayla gave him a serious look. "You explain why, and you *never* ask something like this again."

"I can't get the thought out of my head that Zeal

wants something from those kids. I don't know what it is or why he would, but because of what he said that day, that feeling is there." Chase looked out across the city. "I want to be the only person who knows who and where they are—no files—no data—just in case. We've seen how slimy he is, if Zeal somehow got access to your—"

"Okay."

"Really?"

"Yes, but only because I trust you." Ayla looked down toward the building. "I'm going to erase all mention of them and reset my memory so bare with me. When you think about them, all I'll hear is a big bundle of nothing, so don't worry about that either." She smiled. "You owe me big time, buster."

"I owe you for more than this."

"You're damn right."

Chase was happy to know how much Ayla trusted him. It made sense that since he trusted in her to aid him in battle, she could do the same, but erasing actual memories was an entirely different thing.

He may have lost Marin, but he was happy to be able to call Ayla his friend.

With Ayla and the team—

He wasn't completely alone.

Ayla shut her eyes and her image glitched for a second.

"Ayla? You okay?"

"Weird, I don't remember us coming here." She flew in front of Chase. "So, what is it we're doing right now?"

"Thank you for trusting me."

"What? Duh, obviously I trust you." She flicked a finger between the two of them. "Partners!"

"Well," He crossed his arms. "We've got ourselves a lunch date with the team—I hope it's shawarma."

"I meant after that."

"We need to try to find out what happened to Marin.

See if we can recover—anything. Even if she really didn't survive the fall, Alyx is still out there somewhere." He looked up to the facility, now visible above the city. "After that, we're going to figure out where Zeal is and put his ass behind bars."

"You think we can?"

"We already kicked his butt once. Should be simple enough to do it again, especially if I've got the team behind me."

"Aw, look. Already a big team player. The first Interceptor has some big plans."

"Oh, shut it." Chase moved to the opposite side of the building and took a breath.

He smiled before he hopped off toward the city below.

"WOO-HOO-HOO-HOOOO!"

He may have been the first Interceptor, but he couldn't wait to see how many more there would be.

The End.

Check out the other novels written by Cameron Stewart Miller:

Continue The Intercepting Fate Saga:

Intercepting Fate - Book One:
Extinction Virus

The greatest hero the world has ever known is dead, and a new strain of the Extinction Virus is on the horizon.

After Rhys York, a young boxer from the slums of Sellea City puts his life on the line during a raging house fire, he earns himself an opportunity to become a hero. A team of technologically enhanced heroes known as Interceptors are holding tryouts to find their newest member, but becoming a hero is anything but simple. Along with his best friend Kieran, Rhys battles it out against hundreds of potential recruits in order to become not only the world's newest hero but also the new partner to the most advanced AI in existence, Ayla.

Everyone may dream of one day being a hero that the world can look up to, but Rhys has different goals. Being a hero is great, but getting revenge against the monster that murdered his parents would be even better. Luckily, Rhys's goal lines up with the goal of the Interceptors as the man who killed his parents also happens to be the team's greatest foe, a man known only as Zeal.

A Swashbuckling Adventure:

Scallywags

Is this ship sinking?

That's what Finn thought right before learning one of the most closely guarded pirate secrets ever whispered across the seas.

When Finn was just a boy, his sleepy village was ravaged by a band of horrific pirates. The destruction they left behind was nothing compared to what they had taken – Finn's mother. After years of wondering what happened to her, Finn finds an opportunity to set out in search of his long-lost mother with some help from the most notorious pirate captain to sail the seas, Captain Fortune Palmer.

Finn's only problem is that Fortune isn't exactly what he'd imagined from all the stories he'd heard.

With his furry companion by his side, Finn sets out into the exciting and dangerous world of swashbuckling adventure. Between Pirate Hunters, scorned ex-lovers, and ancient warriors with magical treasure, Finn has his hands full as he works to discover what became of his mother the day she was taken while also proving his worth to his legendary captain.

An Adventure Tale For Younger Readers:

The Glass Flowers

The Travelling Islands

Mahlurma, Cerulea, Flurris, Mulos, and Voxal. After two young boys find themselves transported to this strange new world, they embark on a journey to find their way home. The adventure won't be easy, because getting home means a trip to all of the islands, each stranger than the last. From occasionally wise frog wizards, dishonourable hog kings, and hungry harpy ladies, Wake and Desi must rely on each other and the kooky friends they make on their quest.

In this heartfelt tale, Wake and Desi must each learn what it truly means to grow up, and just how important it is to protect the vibrant nature of the world before it's too late.

A Raunchy Heist Comedy For Adults:

Getting Locked Down

On what was supposed to be the happiest day of his life, Brain Berkley gets ditched at the altar by his fiancee, Sarah for one of the douchiest guys around.

Sappy, I know, but a chance meeting with a mysterious and exciting woman known as Holliday leads Brian into a life he never would have pictured for himself, a life of crime. The neurotic young man has to deal with a woman that's way out of his league, a childhood best friend turned police detective, and the heist of a lifetime, all while Brian does his best to not brown his trousers.

Brian and Holliday may have only just met, but if things don't go as planned then they might be spending the rest of their lives together, whether they want to or not.